SANDCASTLE KISSES

KRISTA LAKES

ZIRCONIA PUBLISHING, INC.

ABOUT THIS BOOK

When Isabel Baker agreed to moonlight as a bartender at a private party, she never imagined she'd get anything more than tips. However, on this resort island, nothing was ever that simple.

After tending bar with the deliciously handsome Noah who was flown in for the party, Izzy realized that she was about to break her number one rule: never fall for a tourist. But with his quick wit, charming smile and passion for marine life, Noah was the kind of guy that she couldn't resist. At the end of the night, she barely managed to turn him away from coming home with her.

Noah had only come to the island for one of Jack Saunders' famous parties. Yet once he met Izzy, he couldn't bring himself to leave. After one steamy night together, he knew that he would do almost anything to keep her.

Theirs should have been an easy love story, complete with a happily ever after. Except Noah was also moonlighting as a bartender that night and his true identity threatened Izzy's research. When his billion-dollar company and her marine research project collide, their entire relationship crumbles into the sand. Will they be able to rebuild their beautiful sandcastle together, or will it be washed away by the rising tide, forever just a memory?

~

"Did you know that my back porch has the best view on the island?" he asked quietly. I smiled. The man knew how to change a subject.

"Is that so?"

"Best view on the island." He crossed his arms with a smug smile.

"And you've been everywhere on the island to check this?"

Noah grinned, standing up and offering me his hand. I couldn't refuse the opportunity to touch him, so I took it and followed him out onto the back porch. He only let me go so that he could close the door behind us.

I leaned up against the railing, looking up at the moon. Her silver light reflected down on the ocean waves, turning their white tips bright. The sky was dark purple now, and the air was humid, dark, and full of promise.

"Yup, definitely the best view on the island," Noah whispered, making me turn. He wasn't looking at the night sky or the ocean. He was looking at me. It was slightly cheesy, but I enjoyed the compliment.

Noah moved forward, gathering me up in his arms. The masculine scent of his light cologne was exhilarating. His mouth slowly slanted to mine, sending small thrills up and down my spine. He went further, tasting me with his tongue like I was something to be savored. A low moan escaped my lips as he pulled me closer to him, his arms strong and demanding around me. His kiss was sweeter than heaven and hotter than hell.

I didn't want to fall for another tourist. *You're not falling*, I told myself. *You're simply enjoying.* I knew he was going to leave and I would be sad. But I would also be far more disappointed if I missed this. His kiss was insistent, intoxicating, and driving me insane. I wanted to melt into him and let him melt into me. I wanted to kiss every inch of his skin. *Every* inch.

I had never been so turned on by a kiss before. It was as if Noah knew everything I loved in a kiss and was delivering and then some. I had never felt this sort of connection with another human being before. I didn't want to get hurt, but I wasn't going to miss this either. *Just one last tourist...*

Don't forget to sign up for <u>my newsletter</u>! You'll be the first to see my new covers, comment on new books of mine, and always know when books are available for free or on sale!

AUTHOR'S NOTE

Author's Note: This book takes place at the same time as
<u>Saltwater Kisses</u>, but is completely stand-alone.

CHAPTER 1

peered out of my dirty car window at the big mansion and had to consciously raise my jaw back up off my chest. I knew houses like this populated the island, but I hadn't actually been this close to one before now. Perfect white marble columns were flanked by lush tropical greenery, and scenic balconies hung out at regular intervals. The place was huge. Grandiose. Palatial. It belonged in a movie. And according to my roommate, it was actually one of the smaller mansions of the island. Key Island was the home of two extremely exclusive resorts, a smattering of multimillion dollar homes, and some locals to help run it all. The island was known as *the* island for people with more money than they could spend.

I shook my head as I eased my ancient little Corolla away from the circle of expensive cars in the driveway. My boss hadn't told me much about the job, just to show up and tend bar. I didn't even know who was officially even throwing it. He said there was a place for me to park to the side of the house and then to find Rachel.

Lamborghinis, Maseratis, and Jaguars lined the roundabout in front of the house, and the worst part was that most of them were dirty. These people used ridiculously expensive cars as their everyday mode of transportation on the island. If using my entire research grant as a way to get to a party wasn't the epitome of wealth, then I wasn't sure what was.

I followed a delivery truck into a little parking lot off to the side of the house. It had an easy slope up to the big doors of a kitchen and was shaded from view of the house by palms and bushes. At least my little car didn't look quite as out of place as I parked it next to a sensible little blue Honda that was only a year or two younger than mine.

I pulled the keys from the ignition and checked my hair and makeup one last time in the rear-view mirror. My strawberry blonde hair was pulled back in a neat ponytail but with cute little tendrils that framed my face. My hair was now mostly blonde after being in the sun and ocean all day, but I thought it suited me.

My eyeliner was perfect and smooth, making my green eyes pop. I hadn't bothered to try and cover up the smattering of freckles across my cheeks, trusting in my old college roommate who said they were cute. She had taught me how to do my makeup in college and had gone on to become a professional makeup artist, so I figured she had to know what she was talking about.

I practiced a flirtatious smile one more time, checking my teeth in the mirror. With the top button of my white shirt just low enough to display cleavage but not appear slutty, I got out of the car. I tugged on my little black vest until it was straight and took a deep breath. Black pants and some sensible shoes completed my bartender outfit. I hoped I looked cute enough to get some good tips.

The tropical air of the Caribbean island was warm and

humid against my skin. It was late afternoon, and the sun was just starting its slow descent down the sky toward blue waters. Birds chirped in the trees, and the beat of dance music started and stopped as someone inside the house worked on getting the sound system set. I felt a tingle of excitement run down my spine. This was going to be a good night.

Just inside the double doors of the kitchen, I found a woman directing traffic. She had on an expensive gray suit, and her dark brown hair was pulled up into a neat bun. Small square glasses were perched on the end of her nose as she peered down at a clipboard and tapped a pen against her lips.

"Are you Rachel?" I asked, stepping up to her. Hers was the only name my boss had given me. She smiled warmly and glanced down at her clipboard.

"Yes. You must be Isabel Baker," she greeted me warmly. I nodded and shook her hand. A man with a keg on a dolly nearly ran me over before Rachel pulled me out of his way. "That goes upstairs on the patio!"

"Do I follow the keg, then?" I asked, my gaze trailing after the man with the keg. Rachel shook her head.

"Nope. You go down to the 'Man Cave.'" She rolled her eyes slightly at the reference, but her smile told me she just thought it was a silly name. "The boys requested to have a real bartender down there tonight. That's where the party will be."

"Oh." I felt a bubble of nerves. This place was incredibly fancy. I hoped I was up to their rich standards. I could feel my palms beginning to sweat.

"Don't worry about them. They just want to relive their glory days," Rachel said warmly, referencing what had to be billionaires like they were her little brothers. "Just don't let them get away with too much. Have fun and don't worry about the booze. Just keep filling up their glasses and smiling, and they'll be happy campers."

"Glasses filled. Got it," I replied.

"If they give you any trouble, just let me know." The dark-haired woman smiled at me and handed me a form to sign. "This is a standard non-disclosure agreement. Your boss said you'd be fine with it."

I quickly scrolled through the form. It seemed pretty straight forward. *Don't tell people who you met here or what they said.* I could understand that famous people wouldn't want to be outed on their vacations or have their drunken ramblings posted across the internet. Signing was easy enough. I handed her back the papers.

Rachel tucked my form behind several others. "Besides that, I'll pay you at the end of the night. Any questions?"

"Just where the 'Man Cave' is," I answered. Rachel's smiled broadened.

"Down that hallway, and then you'll see stairs on your left. Follow the sounds of the boys from there, and you'll find the bar. Remember, have fun. Just tell the guy in the Hawaiian shirt that you're the bartender," she said as a smirk passed over her face at mentioning the Hawaiian shirt.

"Okay, thanks!" I said, but she was already back to her clipboard and chasing after a man wearing a catering uniform. I shook my head. She reminded me of my mom chasing after my little brother and his friends at a birthday party.

I followed Rachel's directions, easily found the stairs, and descended down. "Man Cave" was an excellent term for the room. A tattered but comfortable-looking couch sat in front of a TV big enough to fit in a theater. I could see all sorts of game consoles plugged in and neatly arranged in a massive entertainment system. There was a much-loved pinball machine in the corner and cozy chairs were scattered through the room. The bar took up the far wall, all wooden and shiny with various neon signs overhead. I could see another adjacent room where the DJ equipment was set up. Two men, one blonde and one with sandy hair, were the only party guests I could see so far.

When I stepped from the bottom stair, a large man stepped directly into my path, his arms crossed and an unhappy look on his face. I gulped hard and looked up at his piercing blue eyes. He looked like a sword: thin, limber, and deadly as hell. Then I noticed the brightly patterned shirt with red parrots and blue drinks. It didn't look right on him. It was like a tiger wearing a tutu.

"Um, I'm the bartender," I squeaked. Somehow the man grew taller. Scarier. He was the big bad wolf from the fairytales and he was going to eat me alive. "The woman upstairs told me to tell the guy wearing the Hawaiian shirt..." my voice faltered.

"Quit scaring the poor girl," someone from the party said, putting a hand on Hawaiian-shirt's shoulder. Hawaiian-shirt winked at me, allowing a hint of a smile peek through his tough facade. I nearly giggled with relief.

"Don't mind Dean. He's just mad that we made him dress up for the occasion," my savior said. "I'm Jack. The bar's this way."

"Izzy," I replied. "Nice to meet you."

I slipped behind the bar and promptly ran into a solid mass of man muscle. I watched in horror as our collision spilled the glass of ice in his hand down the front of his shirt.

"Oh crap! I'm so sorry," I apologized, reaching for some

napkins. I found a dry bar towel and held it out to him. He dabbed at his black t-shirt and laughed.

"Don't worry about it. At least it was just ice," he said and handed me back the towel. "I'm Noah. I'm going to be helping you out tonight."

He held out his hand to shake mine. It was warm and strong. My eyes traced from his hand, up perfectly sculpted biceps to a strong jaw and dark hair. His eyes were what made me lose my train of thought, though. They were robin's egg blue and held depths that made my knees weak. Words left my brain. He was flipping gorgeous.

He picked up a new glass and put fresh ice in it to finish making his drink. Vodka, Sprite, some grenadine, and a cherry on top. *A bit girly*, I thought, keeping my face straight.

"A Naughty Shirley for the man of the hour," he said, handing the completed drink across the bar to Jack. Jack took a big sip and let out a sigh of happiness.

"Best bartender ever," he said, winking at me.

"The woman upstairs didn't say anything about having someone else," I said. The bar was barely big enough to hold both of us. We were going to be running into one another all night. Taking another look at him, though, I didn't really mind that idea.

"The guys brought me in special. I used to be their bartender when we were in college." Noah grinned at me.

"All right." I grinned back and pulled out an empty beer pitcher. I had a couple of crumpled ones in my pocket that I threw in it and set it out on the counter. "What side of the bar do you want?"

"I'll take this side," Noah said, inclining his head to the left.

"Barkeep!" Jack called out. "Sex on the Beach next, if you don't mind."

"You know, you really have to buy me dinner first," Noah told him with a wink, pulling out a bottle of peach schnapps. Despite being a seasoned bartender, hearing the words "sex on the beach" come from the mouth of a devastatingly handsome man made my insides tingle.

"Make me an Angel's Tit, Noah." The blonde man Jack had been talking to leaned up against the bar. I snickered slightly.

"Any real drinks?" I teased.

"With these two?" Noah laughed. "Not likely. The reason I was their favorite bartender was because I was the only one who could make the drinks girly enough for them!"

I giggled, already feeling the energy of the night. Jack tossed a five dollar bill into the tip jar after Noah handed him his drink. I grinned at him. With guests like these, the night was going to be hilarious- and profitable.

"So," I said, pulling out the crème de cocao for Noah to make the blonde man's drink. "You're Noah, you're Jack, the guy at the door is Dean, and you are?" I looked expectantly at the handsome blonde man. If I knew their names, I would make better tips.

The three men looked at one another, silent for a second, and then started laughing.

"You don't know who he is?" Noah asked in disbelief.

"No..." I frowned and looked at him closer. He looked slightly familiar, but given that he was Hollywood movie-star handsome, it was probably that I had seen him on TV. "Should I?"

"This is my house. Jack here is just borrowing it." The blonde man smiled. I felt his eyes practically burn into me, daring me to remember. "Does that help?"

Think, think... "I got nothing."

The three men laughed again, and somehow they seemed to relax even more.

"Bob. His name's Bob," Jack grinned. "I guess you don't know Noah's or my last names?"

"If I didn't know his first name, how the heck am I supposed to know your *last* names?" I reasoned with him. His grin got bigger. "Why, are you guys famous or something?"

"Or something," Noah said, handing "Bob" his completed Angel's Tit. "Bob" tossed a ten dollar bill into the tip jar.

Two more men entered the man cave, getting past Hawaiian-shirt Bodyguard Dean with a nod. One was tall and slender with messy honey-colored curls that looked perfect for tangling fingers in. The other was portly and pale, the lines of his face suggesting that the sour look was his usual, permanent expression. His suit looked expensive, but it didn't fit him right and it looked out of place among the other guests' casual t-shirts and shorts.

"Joe!" Jack called out, hurrying over to shake the attractive man's hand. "Joe" got a very confused look on his face.

"Dude, this is Paul..." "Joe" said, patting Jack's shoulder as if he were a confused child. "You've met him before."

Jack rolled his eyes. "No, *you're* Joe. Our bartender doesn't know who we are." Jack grinned as "Joe's" eyes lit up as he got it.

"The fake name game? I love it. I guess he's still Paul, then." "Joe" inclined his head at the heavy-set man bee-lining his way to the bar. "Who's everybody else?"

"I already introduced myself as Jack. Same with Noah. But "Bob" did not."

"Lucky Bob, then. Noah's here? Awesome." Joe turned to the bar, and I felt his eyes do a once over down my body.

"Lucky Noah, actually." At least the last part was quiet enough that I could imagine he hadn't meant me to hear it.

"Give me some of that 1954 Mccallan scotch, sweetheart," Paul said." And don't be stingy." His eyes slid down the opening of my shirt like he owned me. I fought the urge to button up. Hopefully he tipped as well as his friends.

I poured him a generous glass of the amber liquid and set it on the counter. He took one small sip, a smile crossing his thin lips before slamming the rest of it down. I tried not to look horrified. Scotch, especially a bottle that probably cost around three grand, should not be slammed back like a shot. It would be like using a Monet as toilet paper.

"One more, honey," Paul rasped. He coughed slightly at the alcohol burning his esophagus. I guess when you had rich friends, it was tempting to use their nice things in a way you wouldn't normally. I tried to forgive him a little, but it was hard. "If you want some fun later..." He winked and dropped a quarter in the tip jar.

I poured a modest glass, and this time he picked it up and sipped rather than chugging. He gave me that thin-lipped smile that made my stomach curdle a little and went to sit on the couch with "Joe" and "Bob." Jack was starting up a game of some sort on the giant TV screen. Paul turned down an offer for a controller, looking at the black plastic like it might bite him.

"Don't mind him," Noah said, leaning up on the bar beside me. "He's usually pretty harmless. I can't believe Lo-- I mean "Joe"--brought him, though."

"He's not a friend of Jack's?" I asked, wiping down the empty Naughty Shirley glass.

"Not really." Noah shook his head. "He's a lawyer. He's helped us all out at some point or another. I'm just surprised he came. This isn't exactly his type of party."

I looked over at the man on the couch, sipping away on his scotch and glaring at the TV. I could see him at a loud club, leering at the girls, and telling them all how terribly important he was. Sitting on a couch with a bunch of barely-thirty-somethings playing *Halo* didn't exactly fit him.

I shook the beer pitcher, rattling the quarter from Paul. "At least he's a good tipper."

Noah laughed, putting his hand on my shoulder. It was like sexual lighting hit me. Heat flooded my stomach, and if I were less of a lady and more a caveman, I would have thrown him over my shoulder and found a bedroom some-where. I had no idea it was even possible to have that strong a connection just by someone casually touching my shoulder.

I glanced up at Noah, wondering if he felt it too, but he just smiled down at me like he was actually just interested in the tip jar. Except those eyes. They held a blue fire that told me he had felt something too, despite what the rest of his face said.

He cleared his throat, releasing my shoulder and getting a cup of Malibu and Coke for himself. "So, you live here on the island?"

"Yeah." I grabbed one for myself. Rachel *did* say to have a good time. "You just here for the party?"

Noah nodded. "I'm here for a couple of days. My schedule is pretty open, though."

"If you want, I'd be happy to show you around the island. I mean, if "Bob" doesn't want the honor," I offered. Noah's face split into a grin. He nodded and opened his mouth to speak, but a new guest cut him off.

CHAPTER 2

"Hello, Party People!" A man that resembled Jack stepped off the bottom stairs wearing an obnoxiously bright orange Hawaiian shirt. "Looking good, Dean," the man said, patting the big bodyguard on the chest. Dean rolled his eyes.

"Oh, look, my brother is here," Jack said blithely, hitting pause on his game and rising to his feet. "Noah, Izzy, hide the booze so there's some for everybody else."

"Hey, big bro. Love you too." The mini-Jack grinned and came up to the bar. "The usual please, Noah."

"Your name tonight is 'Sam'," Noah told him, pulling out several kinds of liquor. "Izzy here doesn't recognize us."

"Sam's" face went blank for a moment, as though the name meant something to him, but then he put on a dazzling, fake smile. "Seriously?"

"Yup. This is "Bob" and "Joe's" idea, but go with it." Noah pointed to each man to name him. "Jack, Paul and I are already outed."

Sam thought for a moment then grinned. "Let's make it even more interesting. If you figure out everyone's name by the end of the night, I'll give you..." He opened up his wallet and counted his cash. I was expecting it to be around $20. "Two thousand dollars. No cheating and looking it up on your phone. Real detective work. Don't skimp on the cherries, Noah."

I nearly dropped my drink. *Two thousand dollars!* For figuring out some soon-to-be-drunk men's names. I worked in a bar with tourists who loved this game; this was going to be easy.

I leaned up against the bar, making sure he could see the cleavage in my shirt. "And if I don't?"

"You have to go out on a date with me."

"Sam" was cute. Even if I lost, it wasn't going to be the worst night in the world. At least it wasn't a date with Paul. I felt Noah stiffen slightly as he set the amaretto down hard on the counter. *Jealousy?* Nah, he hadn't known me for more than an hour.

"Deal." I reached out my hand and Sam gave it a firm squeeze. "But just the guys who are here now. Just Bob, Joe, and Sam."

"Fair enough." Sam grinned.

"Here's your Screaming Orgasm, *'Sam'*," Noah said, his voice slightly flat. "Sam" grinned and took a big sip.

"You always know the way to my heart," he said to the bartender. Noah rolled his eyes.

"I didn't think Screaming Orgasms usually came with cherries," I said, looking at the drink that was normally a shot. He held a good-sized tumbler of the layered drink with cherries dotting the surface.

"Sam" picked one up with his fingers, put it neatly between his teeth and split it open. "But a screaming orgasm is the best way to pop a cherry."

I felt my cheeks heat. I had walked right into that one.

"Noah, Izzy!" Jack called out. "More drinks!"

I turned from "Sam" to see Noah ready with a fresh Naughty Shirley and something with an inordinate amount of whipped cream. "For 'Bob'. I'll have 'Joe's' ready in a second."

I took the two drinks and carefully maneuvered out from behind the bar and over to the game area. The current match ended just as I arrived, going to the award screen. The "OwenedU" had won and "Bob" was up and doing a victory dance.

"Here you go, Jack," I said, handing him his Naughty Shirley. "And here's your drink, *Owen*."

Owen's dancing stopped and he turned, his face dropping. "So you do know who we are?"

"Owen was actually a guess, *OwenedU*," I said. He sank into his chair and groaned. "But thanks for the confirmation. One down, two to go." I gave him a smile as he took his drink. He got whipped cream on his nose as he tasted it. I went back to the bar and got the drink Noah had ready. "Joe's?" Noah nodded. "Sam" raised his glass in salute to my first name.

The boys were back in a furious battle, and this time I didn't have any hints on the other two gamertags. I was determined that "Joe" was going to be my next discovery. I had a feeling "Sam" was going to be the hardest, since he was the one paying me and benefited from me losing. Plus, from Noah's earlier almost slip, I knew "Joe's" real name started with a Lo- sound, but that could be Logan, Louis, Loren, Lou, or even a last name.

I grinned as I came up behind them. The match was close. I had played Xbox enough with my little brother to know how to read the game. This was almost too easy.

"Joe. Drink for Joe." I called out. The three men were so

intent on their game that no one responded, which was exactly what I wanted.

I called out again, louder this time. No response. I grinned wider.

I waited until the play clock dropped lower. OwenedU and JACKedUP were tied in kill counts with GUEST hot on their heels. It was crunch time for them now, and that was precisely when I stepped in front of the TV screen.

"Drink for Joe," I said as innocently as I could. Owen swore, and Jack craned his neck to look around me. "Joe" nearly fell out of his seat trying to see the screen. I held the drink up higher, blocking more of the game.

"Just take the damn drink, Logan!" Jack hissed before realizing his mistake. He let the control drop to his lap, and he looked up at me, eyes narrowed in speculation as the game ended. Owen won the match again. "You did that on purpose, didn't you?"

"Maybe. Your brother bet me I couldn't get everyone's name by the end of the night, and now he's the only one left with a pseudonym." I handed Logan his drink, moving away from the TV.

Jack raised his eyebrow at me and looked over at his brother. "Just first names?"

I nodded, surprised at how much they wanted to keep their identities secret from me.

"If you can get his name out of him, I'll match whatever he offered you."

My jaw nearly hit the floor. Four thousand dollars if I could just get one more name. Holy freaking cow, was this night suddenly very profitable. I had hoped to get maybe an extra hundred dollars and a nice little paycheck for working this evening, and here I was with an opportunity to get four grand.

"Are you sure? I mean, he offered two thousand dollars, and I don't want to put you in a tight spot," I said.

"Just two?" Jack frowned. He yelled across the room at his brother, "You're getting cheap, bro!"

"Sam" just grinned at him from the bar where he was talking with Noah.

"What are we calling him anyway?" Jack asked.

"Sam," I told him, picking up a couple of empty drink cups. Jack laughed.

"Oh, I bet he loves that. Sam was the name of his girl-friend in middle school."

"She was not my girlfriend!" "Sam" yelled at Jack, unfor-tunately sounding exactly like a middle-schooler.

"Right, that's why you cried-- ouch, man!" Jack stopped his teasing as Owen smacked his arm.

"I know it's your party, but I don't want you two to brawl again. Especially over that. Leave it," Owen warned. Owen's blue eyes darkened as he stared Jack down. Jack glared at him for a moment and then shrugged.

"Rematch?" Jack asked, changing the subject. The tension in the room lightened again as they started up a new game and the sound of gunfire filled the "Man Cave."

As I headed back to the bar, three more men came into the basement. Dean gave them each the evil eye as they passed under his careful watch, but they just came in like they were used to him. They joined the group on the couch, filling the fourth spot and starting to shout and laugh.

Noah and I started getting busy. The newcomers wanted drinks, and luckily they weren't all girly Noah specialties. Two local girls, Lana and Rosie, came in with platters full of food and began wandering around the room offering up the tasty treats.

It was a real party now. I grinned at Noah as party-goers

kept coming up to the bar and requesting drinks. Noah and I worked in tandem as if we had always worked together. It was almost like we were dancing behind the bar. I would reach for the ice, brushing up against him as he went to open the chest for me. We'd reach for matching bottles on the shelf, our fingers caressing for a brief second. Every touch sent electricity crackling over my skin.

"Can you make me a Climax Cocktail?" I called out to him. He shot me a naughty grin.

"Anytime, Izzy," he said with a wink. "But I'm going to need more whipped cream."

Several of the guests laughed, getting in on the naughty drinks and starting to make up their own to keep us busy. I could have sworn they started looking up drinks on their phones just so that they could ask for them and have us shout them across the bar at one another.

"Izzy, can you get me a Redheaded Slut?"

"Sure, but I need to give these guys some Blue Balls first." That one got a nice chuckle from my male audience.

"Screaming Orgasm and Between the Sheets. And the Slow, Comfortable Screw are ready." Noah managed to keep a straight face, which was better than I was doing.

"Sit on My Face, Panty Dropper and a Gin Tonic," I called out, glad for the normal drink. The patrons all turned and looked at Logan as he picked up his non-dirty named drink.

"What? I like Gin and Tonics," he said with a laugh.

It was getting later into the night, and things finally started to slow down again. The TV held most of the crowd's attention. A huge whiteboard displayed a chart with everyone's names in a tournament bracket. It hung on the wall behind the couch, and the various teams were yelling and cheering on their teammates and friends. Unfortunately for me, "Sam" had decided not to play and didn't have his name on the board.

"You want to tell me what 'Sam's' real name is?" I asked Noah as we tucked empty bottles into a very full trashcan. It was all top-shelf liquor, and I didn't even want to think about how much money had been drunk by the party-goers.

"That would be cheating," Noah said. "And as much as I would like to save you from a date with him, I am not a cheater."

I leaned back against the wall. Noah's black shirt fit him perfectly. It accented his muscled arms and chest and made the blue in his eyes pop, even in the neon lights. I wished for a moment that it was his name I was trying to learn. If it was a date with him that was the penalty, it would be worth losing the money.

CHAPTER 3

"*N*oah, have you seen Dean?" "Sam" said, running up to the bar. "Paul's being an ass and harassing the caterers. I need a little backup."

I glanced at the empty stairs. "He had to take a guest out to throw up. I thought he'd be back by now," I answered.

Noah was already walking out of the bar, anger flashing in his eyes. I felt a shiver run through me. I was glad I wasn't the one he was headed toward with that expression on his face.

I followed "Sam" and Noah upstairs and into the foyer with the main stairs to the rest of the house. Paul had his meaty fist wrapped around Lana's slender arm, and she looked terrified.

"Please," she said, her voice shaking as she tried to stay calm. "I need to go back downstairs and..."

"Paul, I told you to lay off her." "Sam" growled, pulling Paul off the girl. Paul stumbled into the wall, obviously drunk. Free from his grasp, Lana twisted away from him and toward the front door, escaping to freedom.

"Get off of me," Paul slurred, throwing a punch that "Sam" easily ducked. I could see why he wanted backup. Paul wasn't going down without a fight.

"Come on, Paul. I think you've had enough," Noah said. He put himself on the other side of Paul so that he and "Sam" could each take an arm. "It's time for you to go take a rest."

Paul took a couple of cooperative steps before he saw me. I swallowed hard and wanted to run. The greasy feeling of his eyes on me told me that I should have followed Lana out. I should have stayed at the bar.

"How about you boys let *her* put me to bed? She looks ready for me," Paul leered, and I felt like I needed a shower.

"Nope, you get us. Owen's got a nice room all ready for you upstairs. The lady isn't interested," "Sam" said, taking his arm.

"Shut up, Robbie. Nobody asked you," Paul snapped, pulling his arm away. I met "Sam's" eyes as we both registered the name. "Sam", or rather Robbie's face fell. This wasn't how I wanted to win the bet.

"Thanks, man." Robbie sighed and shrugged his shoulders at me and continued to try to coax Paul up the stairs.

"No." Paul stopped in his tracks, his suit hanging in unattractive folds. He had spilled something on his shirt. "*She* needs to earn the tip I gave her. Besides, she *wants* it. Just look at her."

I couldn't stop the heat from rising from my stomach to my cheeks. The insult to my honor burned. My fist balled up but my feet refused to move. I wanted to slug his pasty little head in.

Noah stepped in front of Paul, blocking his path to me. Noah was somehow bigger, more intimidating than he had been down in the bar. He leaned forward and whispered something in Paul's ear, something that made the older man go even paler. Paul's round chin bobbed as he swallowed nervously.

"Now, go upstairs with Robbie," Noah growled. Robbie took Paul's arm, guiding him to the stairs I was unfortunately standing next to. I wanted to step away from him, but I didn't want to give him the satisfaction of knowing I was afraid of him. So, I stood my ground.

As the drunk man came closer, he reached out his grubby mitt and squeezed my chest. I gasped and stepped back, but Noah's fist was on Paul's cheek faster than I could raise my hand to slap him. Paul sprawled out on the floor and held his palm to his cheek, shock in his eyes.

"Get upstairs." Noah's voice held a threat I knew Paul didn't want to test. He scampered to his feet and hurtled up the stairs with Robbie tailing after him.

"Nice shot, Noah. I'll make sure he gets to a bathroom, or Owen will throw a fit." Robbie turned. "I'll come find you at the bar to pay up, Izzy."

"Are you okay?" Noah asked. His voice was low and soft as he put his hands on my shoulders. I could feel myself trembling against him. I wasn't quite sure why; I dealt with drunks on a regular basis at the bar, but I guessed it was just the suddenness of it all that had shaken me.

"Yeah," I said, giving him a wobbly smile. "Not the first time I've been hit on at a bar. Remind me to stay on your good side. How'd you hit him so fast anyway?"

One side of Noah's mouth went up in a small half-smile as he bent down to look me in the eyes. His blue eyes held nothing but concern, the edges of a flame still there but not directed at me. I felt giddy this close to him, his hands warm on my shoulders. If I leaned forward just a little, I could've kissed him.

"I used to box. Never professionally or anything. I just liked the exercise." His lips curved into a stronger smile as he looked at me. I could see now where he got those beautifully sculpted arms and chest. He was so close I could practically taste his kiss. A kiss from him sounded wonderful. It would certainly make me feel better.

"Where's Paul?" Owen asked, breaking the tension between us. His eyes flashed daggers, and anger filled his voice. Dean was one step behind him, looking deadly. I almost felt sorry for Paul.

"Upstairs. Robbie's with him." Noah straightened and dropped one of his hands, but thankfully left one on my shoulder.

"Are you okay?" Owen asked, turning to me. "That poor catering girl is pretty shaken up."

"I'm fine. I deal with drunks all the time. He just surprised me is all." I gave him a stronger smile. "I should go check on Lana."

"I'll go with her," Noah volunteered. "You and Dean go make sure Robbie doesn't give Paul a swirly."

Owen nodded, heading up the stairs with Dean. Noah turned back to me, and together we went out to the front porch where Lana and the other caterer, her sister Rosie, were sitting on the porch. Night was deep and dark, but the porch light held them in a protective, warm, yellow light. Rosie had her arm over Lana's shoulder, and as we came out she gave her a squeeze.

"You two okay?" I asked.

Rosie nodded. "I've got her, Izzy.. She's gonna be fine," She squeezed Lana's slim shoulder again. "If it's okay, I'd like to take her home."

"I'll let Rachel know, and I'll make sure you two get your full check," Noah assured her. I knew he would too. There was something in his voice that told me he would pay it out of his own pocket if he had to.

"Thanks." Rosie smiled and pulled Lana up. "Let's get you home."

Lana stood and gave us both an appreciative smile. "Thanks. And thank that other guy for me too."

Noah nodded and we followed them with our eyes as they headed into the parking lot before heading back downstairs ourselves.

I glanced at my watch as we headed back behind the bar. It was a little after two in the morning. Time had flown by. The *Halo* Tournament was over, and Owen had won. Jack met us at the bottom of the stairs, his brows drawn together.

"Is everything okay?"

Noah put a hand on his shoulder. "Yeah. Paul was just a dick. Like usual. Sorry about the bad ending to the party."

"Not your fault. Besides, the party was mostly over anyway." Jack shrugged and looked around the room. Glasses and food were everywhere. "It was still a great sendoff."

"Sendoff?" I asked. "Are you getting married or something?"

Jack laughed. "I suppose you could say I'm getting married to my job. I'm taking over my dad's company in a week, and I won't get another day off until I'm seventy. I even got a nice little bed installed in my office." He grimaced and shook his head as if to clear the thought. "Where's Ro--I mean, where's 'Sam'?"

"*Robbie* is upstairs helping," I said, emphasizing the name.

Jack laughed. "So he lost the bet. Good job. I'll have Rachel put my part on your check. Don't let Robbie stiff you on his share."

And with that he turned back to the TV and started another game of *Halo*.

CHAPTER 4

It wasn't long before Rachel came down the stairs into the 'Man Cave'. I didn't know how she did it, but she looked as fresh and ready as if it were two in the afternoon instead of the morning. Dean hung behind her in the shadow of the stairs, his eyes watching her move through the room. There was something in the way he looked at her, and how she was purposefully ignoring his glances, that made me think there was something between them.

"Thank you for your services, Ms. Baker," Rachel said, handing me a check. The ink was still wet on the extra two-thousand dollars. I was almost afraid to put it in my pocket, as if it might smudge and the bank wouldn't accept it. "You're welcome to go home whenever you're ready."

"The bar's still a disaster area, so I'll clean that up before I go," I said, gesturing to the bar. Cups and bottles were everywhere. Rachel waved a hand dismissively.

"Don't worry about it. I hired a bartender, not a bar-cleaner. I already have custodians arranged to take care of everything in the morning. You've had a busy night. Go on home and get some rest."

"Are you sure?" I asked her. I always took it as part of my job to clean up the bar. To get to go home early and have someone else take care of the part I hated doing was a gift.

Rachel nodded. "Go home. It looks like the boys had a good time, so you did your job well."

"I'll walk you out," Noah volunteered quickly. Rachel smiled at him and then went to go find Jack. He was busy setting up a rematch with Logan on some video game. I waved to the two of them as Noah led me up the stairs.

At the top of the stairs, we ran into Robbie and Owen.

"Here's your prize money," Robbie said, handing over twenty one-hundred dollar bills. "I'll still throw in the date if you're interested, though."

I laughed. "Thanks. I'll keep that in mind." I paused in taking the money. It felt weird to take as much as he was offering, even though he seemed so nonchalant about it. Like it was nothing to hand over two thousand dollars on a stupid bet.

"Take the money," Robbie said, closing my hand around it. "You won it."

I stuffed the money into my pocket, feeling a little strange at holding that much cash. I wondered what he did that he even carried that much cash around. *The island is a millionaire's play-place,* I silently reminded myself. *If he's here, he can afford it.*

"Okay. Thanks." I smiled up at Robbie. "You have a good night. You too, Owen."

"You too. G'night, Noah," Owen said. He took a sip of a drink and waved us out the door. Noah put his hand on the small of my back, guiding me out onto the yellow light of the porch. Insects sung to one another in the night, and I could hear the ocean keeping time for them. Stars peeked out of their dark blanket while the moon glided on silver wings. I loved nights on the island. They were always magical.

"I had a great time working with you," Noah said quietly. I liked the way his hand felt on my back. I didn't take the step off the porch. I didn't want the night to end yet. Especially the part with Noah.

"Me too." I turned and smiled up at him. He smiled back and offered me his arm.

"Can I walk you to your car?"

I took it, feeling the muscles flex. I felt embers deep in my stomach flare to life. I wanted to know what it would feel like to run my fingertips down those arms. How he would look without a shirt... his body pressed to mine...

Before I knew it, we were at my car. I wished I had walked slower, but I knew we had gone at a snail's pace the whole way.

"Thank you. For everything," I said slowly, digging in my pocket for my keys. I took my time.

Noah ran a hand through his short dark hair. The pale sliver of moon accented the lines of his jaw and sparkled in his eyes. "Um, I don't usually do this, but *would* you be interested in coming to my place for drinks?"

Liar, I thought. *I'm sure you have girls over all the time. You're too handsome not to.* Smooth, but not smooth enough. As gorgeous as he was, there was no way I was going to do anything while exhausted and covered in various liquors and whip cream. I shook my head no.

"Oh, okay then. Your place?"

I gave him a gentle shove. "Nice try. Nope. I am covered in sticky."

"So am I..." he laughed. "There's a dirty joke in there, but I'll be the gentleman and not say it."

I imagined myself getting sticky with him. It was a nice thought. A deliciously hot and sticky thought. But not one I was ready to do tonight. My body was just too tired.

I clicked the unlock button on the car and then smacked my forehead with my palm. "I forgot the tip jar!"

Noah grinned. "But I didn't. Here you go." He handed me a neat roll of bills and one quarter.

"Noah..." I eyed the massive roll, seeing mostly fives and tens. "We have to split it. You did most of the work anyway with all the girly drinks."

Noah laughed. The sound was light and floated on the night air like it had wings. "I don't need the money."

"Why not?" I asked. Suddenly it dawned on me. "You're more than just a bartender, aren't you?"

"Yes. But Jack paid me more than enough to tend bar again." He smiled. "I want you to have it. Seriously. Use it for something fun."

"You're sure?" I asked once more before taking the money. It seemed like everyone here was giving me crazy amounts of money tonight.

"Very sure." He leaned forward and gave me a light kiss on the cheek. The touch of his lips fanned the embers in my stomach to an achy burn. I closed my eyes. I wanted to say yes to him, to go with him to his room and let those arms wrap around me, but I knew I should say no. I needed to stay strong. He was handsome, but I didn't need a one night stand.

"Thank you," I whispered. He pulled back and opened the car door for me to get in. A true gentleman.

"Have a wonderful night, Izzy."

I sat down on my imitation leather seats, and he closed

the door. He gave me one last dazzling smile before turning and heading back to the house. I watched his figure outlined by the yellow light of the porch for a moment before starting the car.

The engine mumbled quietly as I pulled out and onto the empty road to get home. It was close enough that I could have walked, but I liked the ease of a car on these late night jobs. I turned onto the main road, my headlights bright against the dark night.

I could still feel his lips on my cheek. He had been funny and charming. No mention of a wife or a girlfriend or anything to give me warning. He had been protective. I nearly hit the brakes to turn around and go back. I wanted to feel those muscled arms encircling me. I wanted to feel those lips again.

No, I told myself firmly. *He's just a tourist. You don't even know his last name. He's going to leave just like they all do. Best not to even get attached.*

I nodded, proud of myself for staying resolute and ignoring the way my heart cried out that I should go back. My head, not my body, was who I needed to listen to. No matter how wonderful he had seemed.

CHAPTER 5

I woke up the next morning with a smile on my face. My dreams had been invaded by an irresistible man with blue eyes and unending charm. The best part was that in my dreams, I didn't have to stop. I didn't have to be responsible, reasonable, or nervous. I could do anything, and everything, that I wanted. Waking up, I was sad to leave my dreams behind. They had been some of the best dreams of my life.

I stretched my hands over my head, looking over to see a neatly made bed in the opposite corner of the room. Brooke was already up, which meant that there was probably some leftover breakfast in the kitchen. Brooke was always good for leaving me breakfast after work nights.

I quickly got ready, running a brush through my hair and finding my wetsuit. Despite my diet of fish and tropical fruit, it was still snug across the hips. *Eh*, I thought, *I don't need to impress the sharks today.* Sunglasses and some sunscreen completed my morning preparations.

I walked quickly to the kitchen and found two deviled eggs waiting for me in the fridge. Brooke made the best deviled eggs, and she knew they were my favorite. I couldn't ask for a better roomie. I stuffed one in my mouth and carried the other out of the kitchen to the back porch.

Outside, the big porch wrapped around the house. To the right was a sandy beach where we had built several holding pens for containing sharks for research or rehabilitation. We had several sheds set up by the pens to hold more equipment and gear.

The house backed out onto the water with a little dock for our two research boats. The building had once been a decently sized home, but Dr. Algos had transformed it into a marine biology research station over twenty years before I had even arrived. The only part of it that actually looked like a house anymore was the outside. The three bedrooms were now for research assistants and their projects, the living room was filled with different sized fish tanks, and the dining room was full of computers and research equipment. Even the kitchen had an attached area where we could prep shark bait.

Dr. Algos was out loading one of the boats. I headed down the dock toward the boat, filling my mouth with the second egg.

"Hi, Izzy," Dr. Algos called out as soon as he saw me. "Good night last night?"

"Hey, Doc. I made awesome good tips. Where are you off to?" I asked.

"Tagging. There have been some hammerheads spotted over by Shark Tooth Rock. Brooke and I going to try and get a transmitter on 'em." Doc straightened from loading the boat and shaded his face with his hand. "You know when Lucas and Devon get back from the mainland?"

He was a tall, lean man with graying hair that he kept cropped close to his head. He had permanent sunglasses lines around his warm brown eyes. His love was the ocean. Sharks, rays, fish, dolphins- if it swam, he studied it. He had been studying marine biology for longer than I had been alive. His love of the ocean was a big part of why I was out here helping him with his research.

"They'll be back tomorrow evening. Devon said his dissertation went well," I told him. "They promise they'll bring as much peanut butter and mainland goodies as they can fit in their suitcases."

"Mmm, peanut butter," Brooke said as she walked past me with her arms full of chum buckets. She somehow made carrying bloody fish look sexy. Some days I hated Brooke. She was possibly the most beautiful person I had ever met. Tall, with legs that stretched into infinity, she also had perfectly sculpted abs and a megawatt smile. The thing was, she knew she was gorgeous, but she only used the advantage at the bars. She was also one of the nicest people I knew, and my best friend and roommate on the island.

Dr. Algos turned back to me. "You're in the pen today, Izzy. Feed and check the pups, and then you can have the rest of the day off. I don't want you doing any more research until we know we'll have assured access to the Grove."

I nodded. "Have you heard anything from the lawyers?"

Doc shook his head. "Nope. I put another call in, but I they haven't responded yet. It looks like the auction date is pushed back again. Try not to worry, okay?"

I smiled and nodded. Not worrying was far easier said than done. The Grove was supposed to be the site of my doctoral project as well as a nature preserve. There was a perfect mangrove outcropping just down the road from the research center. The mangroves grew out on a promontory that stretched out into the ocean making a unique habitat. Numerous species of sharks, fish, and marine life used the mangroves to harbor their young until they were big enough to survive in the open ocean. The only problem was that it was on private property. That hadn't been a problem until the owner, who had given us permission to use it, suddenly died. The land was set to go up for auction.

We teamed up with several other scientists, hoping to buy the property and turn it into a wildlife reserve. The local government wasn't being much help in the process, but we were determined to save the Grove. Unfortunately, it was a prime piece of real estate, and we were going to be cutting it close as it was. The land was due to go up for auction any day now, and I hoped we had enough. If we weren't successful, then the best we could hope for was that the new owner would still allow us access.

Doc already had grant money lined up to investigate how the nursery habitat of mangrove trees influenced the growth of lemon sharks as part of his current investigations. I had already done months of prep and to get it ready. I had risked it, not knowing we would lose access and already started on some of my research. The Grove was perfect for the thesis I had in mind. If the new owner denied us access, then I had to figure out a new project and my work would be for nothing. Dr. Algos' grant money would disappear. It was all dependent on the Grove.

I shook my head, clearing the negative thoughts. There was nothing I could do about it right now, and worrying wasn't going to make it better. I was just offered a day off and I was going to take it. I had a new book I wanted to read and I knew a little patch of beach that was just calling my name.

"You two have fun. Catch lots of sharks," I called out as Brooke and Dr. Algos climbed aboard the small motor boat. Brooke waved as they cast off and headed into the dark blue waters to find their quarry. I watched them disappear toward the horizon for a moment before turning and heading toward the pens.

We had two permanent pens and a third temporary one that we could set up when we did large population counts. They looked a lot like swimming pools, except they were attached to the ocean and filled with sand. Only one had occupants, and they were my favorites.

Sitting quietly on the sandy bottom were two baby nurse sharks. Two baby lemon sharks swam in lazy circles above them. The two lemon sharks were part of a tagging program while the two nurse sharks had been found tangled in fishing line.

I waded into the shallow water, a familiar thrill coursing through my skin. Every time I got in the water with these creatures, my heart would surge with excitement. These little two-foot long babies would soon be the apex predators in the ocean. I waded out to one of the nurse sharks, moving slowly and deliberately. The first was easy to catch and I checked it over to make sure that it was healing appropriately. I loved the rough shark skin against my fingers.

I let it go and found the second, performing the same check. They looked healthy and were putting on weight. A veterinarian would come by in a couple of days and check them out again, but I had a wonderful suspicion that we would be releasing them back into the Grove soon. Yet another reason I wanted the Grove to survive.

I finished checking out the sharks and giving them their feeding. I loved working with the sharks. They were beautiful and deadly, but surprisingly gentle and timid. I had even noticed personality traits the longer I worked with them.

"Bye, guys, see you tomorrow," I told the little sharks as I stepped out of their pool and put their feeding supplies away. They didn't respond, but I didn't care.

Heading back inside, I stripped out of the wetsuit and put on my favorite tankini. Brooke kept trying to convince me to wear one of her itsy-bitsy bikinis, but I liked my more conservative swimsuit choice. I dropped a sundress over my head and grabbed my beach bag. It was time for a relaxing day reading and taking in some vitamin D.

CHAPTER 6

My beach spot was on the same property as the Grove, but since it didn't technically have a new owner yet, I figured it was still safe to use as my tanning spot. I set up my towel on a patch of sand and sat down. From my spot, I could see the edge of the Grove as well as a pristine sandy beach. I loved the Grove. Just being near it made my day better.

A slender woman with dark hair came out of the shadows of the mangroves. She had on khaki shorts with a cute little t-shirt and boots that shouldn't have been in the salty, mucky water of the Grove. She wore an annoyed, sour expression on her face as she headed along a small path back toward the town center. I shook my head at her. Tourists were always doing weird things on the island.

I dug my toes into the sand, feeling the cool damp of deeper sand mix with the hot dry of the top. The waves shushed gently at the shore, whispering soft nothings that I loved to hear. The sky was clear and blue. Like Noah's eyes.

My mind went to the night before and to the dreams I had in the morning. Those eyes were going to fuel my dreams for a while. He was more handsome than was fair for a human being. He was also a tourist. No way I was going to get my heart broken for someone who was going to leave me in a week to return to their real life. I had done the right thing turning him down.

"Hi, Izzy," a deep voice greeted me, throwing me completely off balance. Standing before me in board shorts and a skin tight t-shirt was the very gorgeous Noah. I wasn't sure how he pulled it off, but he was somehow even more attractive today. He took off his dark sunglasses and smiled down at me.

"Hi, Noah," I answered. I ran a hand over my hair, hoping that it wasn't a total disaster. I hadn't planned on meeting a handsome man on a private beach when I left the house this morning. "How are you?"

"Doing great now," he replied. His eyes twinkled as I stood up and brushed the sand from my legs. I wasn't sure if it was just my imagination or if there was an extra warmth in his smile that was just for me. "How about you?"

"Just getting some reading done." I nodded toward the book on my towel. "I have the day off, so I'm just taking it easy. What are you up to today?"

"Just wandering around. Seeing the sights of the island." A thoughtful expression crossed his face, a slight hint of a smile tilting his lips upward. "Would you be interested in some breakfast? There's a little diner down the road that I saw on my way in, and I wanted to try it."

"You mean Adele's? It's fantastic!" I might have sounded too eager, but I didn't care. "Heck yeah, I'm in for breakfast!" I grinned and bent to pick up my stuff. Noah reached for my book as I rolled the towel back up to fit in my bag. Our hands brushed as he gave it to me, sending a warm heat surging through my core.

Once my bag was packed, Noah offered me his arm as though he were escorting me to a ball rather than down a beach. I giggled and took it, feeling like a princess. His arm was solid and warm beneath my fingers. I was glad I was looking forward and he couldn't see me clearly, because a silly grin and a blush were coating my face.

"HEY, IZZY," Adele, the owner, called out as Noah and I walked into the small restaurant. I waved a hello as the door chimed behind us and I went to claim my favorite table. The restaurant was brightly colored and decorated with pink flamingos and parrots. It screamed tourist attraction, but Adele made it homey and warm. I sat down at my favorite table by the window, and Noah followed my lead.

"You've been here a few times, I take it?" he asked with a smile. I laughed.

"Yup. Dom over there owns the bar I work at on weekends, and Adele is his wife. The bar is right next door. This is my favorite place to get breakfast." I slid him a menu. "If you like French toast, Adele makes it from cinnamon rolls."

"Cinnamon rolls? I'm sold. I'm having that." Noah set the menu down and grinned.

"Yeah, it's my favorite. That or the banana-nut crepes."

"Okay, now you're making me rethink my first choice..." He reached for the menu. I put my hand on his to stop him, feeling a quiver in my stomach at his touch.

"Go with the Cinnamon Roll French Toast. Tomorrow you can come back and get the crepes. Or for dinner. Adele serves breakfast all day." I let go of his hand and sat back into my chair.

"This island just keeps getting better and better!" Noah laughed.

Adele came over in her yellow plaid apron and pale yellow dress. I always thought she was what a grandmother should look like. She was all warm curves, hugs, and smiles. It was part of the appeal of eating at Adele's. Not only was there amazing food, but it felt like I was always getting spoiled by a favorite relative by coming there.

"What can I get you folks?" Adele asked.

"Two of my usual. Bacon and scrambled eggs on mine, please," I replied politely.

"Scrambled eggs and sausage links for me. And coffee," Noah added.

"You got it. It'll be right out," Adele promised, taking our menus and bustling off to the kitchen. It was slow now that the breakfast rush was over. The normal waitress must have been on break, so Adele was probably playing both waitress and cook.

"So, what do you do, Noah? Other than tend bar?" I asked, trying to start a conversation.

"I buy distressed properties," he said. A light went out in his blue eyes, like this wasn't something that he enjoyed discussing.

"That sounds... interesting." I was surprised at his lack of enthusiasm. Most people were eager to tell others about their work and what they did.

"Not really. It's actually quite boring," Noah replied, his voice flat. Adele reappeared at our table with a fresh pot of coffee and poured us each a steaming mug. She left the carafe along with a small pitcher of cream. I eagerly added some to my coffee and poured some sugar in as well. Noah took his black.

"You must be good at it," I said once Adele had left.

"Good at what?" Noah looked at me confused, his dark brows meeting in the center of his forehead.

"Distressed properties."

"What makes you think I'm good at it?" His voice held no emotion, and his eyes were blank. He took a sip of his coffee.

"Because no one who is friends with Jack Saunders would be able to do something badly."

Noah frowned slightly. "So you know who Jack is?"

"My roommate adores those tabloid magazines. If she knew that 'New York's most eligible bachelor' was in town, she'd flip her lid." I played with my coffee mug and then looked up at him. "I actually didn't even recognize him until I went home and saw him on the cover of one of her magazines. I am so out of the celebrity loop. If it hadn't been laying on her bed, I never would have made the connection."

"Are you going to tell her?" Noah's blue eyes searched my face.

"Hell no." I set my coffee cup down. "She'd go off to find him, and I'd get stuck doing all her research work!"

Noah laughed, and his face relaxed. The light was back in his eyes. He was a good friend to worry about his buddy like that. I couldn't help but like him just a little bit more.

"So, research work? What do you do?" Noah asked. He leaned in against the table, as if he were actually interested.

"I'm a marine biologist."

"Do you work with dolphins?" Noah's eyes sparkled at the idea.

I shook my head. "Sharks, actually."

"Sharks?" Noah frowned. "Like *Jaws*?" he made a chomping motion with his hands, and I giggled.

"Sharks, yes. Jaws, no. Jaws was a great white shark, and

they typically don't live in the Caribbean," I explained gently.

Noah leaned back in his chair and crossed his arms. "You must not have seen *Jaws Four*, then."

"It's what inspired me to become a marine biologist!" I opened my eyes wide in mock enthusiasm, making him laugh. "It's only the worst movie ever," I said, making a face, and he laughed harder. "I actually mostly study lemon sharks. Not great whites."

"Do they look like great whites?" He gave me a serious look. "Please tell me we're going to need a bigger boat."

I snorted a laugh, covering my mouth with my hand so I wouldn't spit out my coffee. It wasn't like anyone had never made the joke before, but when he said it, it was hilarious. It took me a second to recover and not shoot coffee out my nose.

Adele came by then, and dropped off our food. I took a big inhale of the rising steam before diving into the scrumptious feast. This was why my wetsuit was a little tight, but it was more than worth it. Butter dripped off the fried slices of cinnamon roll. The eggs were covered in cheese, and my bacon was the prime level of crispy. Adele had made the perfect breakfast yet again.

"Holy mother..." Noah said quietly as he chewed his first bite. "Did I die and go to Breakfast Heaven?"

I just grinned at him and dug into my plate. We ate in companionable silence for a few minutes, the food taking both of our attention away from talking.

"Have you ever been bit by a shark then?" Noah asked, his blue eyes concentrated entirely on my face. He pushed his empty plate away and leaned forward in his chair, honestly interested in my profession. It was wonderful to get to talk to him and not be constantly interrupted by drink orders.

"Once, but it was a baby. I didn't even get a good scar out of it."

"I can't imagine being in the water with one of those monsters. They kind of freak me out a little bit." He smiled with just a hint of bashfulness. Like admitting he was afraid of sharks made him somehow less of a man. "How many sharks are in the area?"

"Well, we've recorded about thirteen species. The island actually has one of the highest populations of sharks in the area," I told him.

He paled slightly. "I'm never going in the water again."

"Oh, they're not that bad! Sharks are cool!" I reached out and put my hand on his without thinking. "Haven't you seen Shark Week?"

"Yes. And I've seen all the episodes where people get bitten!"

I rolled my eyes, but I smiled, taking any sting out of my expression. "Fine. I dare you to come swim with me, then. I'll show you the wonders of the deep."

"If my arm gets bitten off, I get yours."

I pretended to think about it for a moment. A movement outside the window caught my eye, and I could see the woman with the khaki shorts from earlier looking in various windows of the local shops.

"You'd look pretty silly with my arm," I told him, wearing a serious face. "I think it would be too short for you."

"Hmm..." He frowned and nodded. "Good point."

"How about I take you on a tour of the research pools sometime? You can see a baby shark, and it won't bite you," I offered.

"Baby sharks just bite you, then?" he asked with mock seriousness.

"Only when you are tagging them and they're mad at you," I said with a smirk.

"Sounds good to me." He grinned at me and then followed my gaze out the window to the woman in khaki shorts.

"Let's get out of here," he said quickly, throwing a fifty dollar bill on the table. Our bill couldn't have been more than thirty dollars even with a generous tip, but I knew Adele wouldn't mind the extra money.

Noah grabbed my hand, a grin spreading across his handsome features as he pulled me out the restaurant and back toward the beach.

CHAPTER 7

oah didn't drop my hand as we walked out of the restaurant. He didn't drop it as we walked out of the town square, or as we meandered down the pathway leading to the beach. I wasn't about to let go either, even though I could feel mine going sweaty and hot. I didn't want to lose our connection.

We crested a small hill to the beach, and I could see the ocean laid out before us. The golden sunshine sparkled on the waves, the white light almost too bright to look at. We stood there for a moment, hand in hand, staring out at the waves.

"How long are you in town for again?" I whispered. I had been thinking the words since we met, but I hadn't found the courage to say them until now. Despite my best intentions, I liked Noah. Really liked him. But he was a tourist and was going to leave as soon as his vacation was done. It was better just not to get attached. I didn't let go of his hand, though.

Noah stared out at the water for a moment before answering, his eyes distant and his voice quiet. "Just a couple more days. I really only came for the party last night." He turned and smiled gently. "You can't say no to a Jack Saunders party."

"He would definitely be a hard man to say 'no' to." I turned to look out at the water again. I loved the way the blue of the sky melded with the blue of the water, obscuring the horizon. I wanted the ocean to go on for forever, and I liked the illusion that it did.

Noah suddenly disengaged our handhold and took off for the water. He sprinted across the sandy beach and ran into the foam of the waves. I hurried after him, afraid he had seen something that needed rescuing. Dolphins had been known to wash up on shore, or even exhausted swimmers.

When I caught up to him, he held up a small bucket with various plastic shovels attached to the handle. They were just cheap, plastic beach toys, but he held them up in victory as though he had rescued a mermaid.

"Look what I saved: The environment!" he exclaimed. His smile was as bright as the sun as he stumbled out of the water and back onto the sandy beach.

"My hero!" I cooed, batting my eyelashes up at him. He grinned even broader.

"I used to play with these all the time. I made the best sandcastles," he said, turning the bucket and shovels over in his hands. I could see a multitude of happy memories shining in his eyes as he played with the toys.

"Me too. I once made one with my dad that could have won a castle-building contest," I said.

Noah grinned at me. "You wanna make one now?"

There was no way I was going to say no. The glint in his eye, the smile, the easy way to get to spend more time with him. Tourist or not, I liked him and I wasn't about to pass up an opportunity to build sandcastles with a handsome man. Besides, it was my day off.

"Only if we can fill the moat with actual water." I crossed my arms, pouting my lips like the moat was a deal breaker.

"What kind of castle would it be without a water-filled moat?" he responded with mock seriousness. I grinned with childlike delight, hurrying over to a sandy spot where we could start building.

I kicked off my shoes, digging in the sand with my hands and feet to start building the foundation for our sandcastle. Noah dug up buckets of wet sand and dumped them in a pile next to the foundation. He moved like an excited kid. Every motion was exaggerated yet purposeful, but it was the grin plastered to his face that told me he was enjoying himself.

Once I had the base for the castle smooth, Noah spread wet sand across it and then used the bucket to pack it down. It took us a couple of minutes, but a strong foundation would make the castle last longer.

I went to fill the bucket with sand, carefully turning it over so that it would maintain its shape. I went to fill another, but Noah gently grabbed the bucket from my hands.

"The secret to a sandcastle is to build down, not up." He smiled and his eyes sparkled with excitement. "If we build down, then we won't risk knocking it over, and it's far more stable."

"Are you secretly a prize-winning sandcastle artist?" I asked, the idea making more sense as I thought about it. If we made a big pile of sand, packed it down, and then started shaping it, the sandcastle wouldn't fall apart because it was already solid.

"Only on weekends," Noah teased.

Together we piled the wet sand on the center of the foundation, packing it down with our hands and giggling as our fingers touched. It was impossible not to run into him working as closely as we were. Our hands would brush as we packed the sand down; our knees would bump against each other as we reached for more sand; our elbows would knock together as we piled the sand higher.

"If we make a tower here, and a door here," Noah explained, pointing to the lumpy sand with his hands. His eyes were bright as he imagined the castle in his mind and used his hands to explain it to me. "Then we can build this part up and make it last longer."

"You sound like an architect," I said with a smile. He gave me a grin that melted my heart. It made him even more attractive that he was excited and involving me.

"I've always had a thing for architecture. I never went to school for it, but in my spare time I like to design things. It isn't what pays the rent, but it's something I enjoy." He turned back to the castle and started to use his hands and the shovel to create the basic structure of the castle.

I watched him for a moment before joining in, admiring the surety of his hands. I had a feeling not many people got to see this side of him. Creative. Happy. He practically glowed with enthusiasm as he guided the sand into a beautiful castle.

"Help me hold this here," he said quietly. He put my hand on the wet sand, his direct touch sending an electric shock of desire straight down my spine. The ache of pure want grew in the pit of my stomach, filling my body with heat. If his hand could have this kind of effect on me, I wanted to know what other parts of his body could do.

Noah didn't seem to feel the same shock, but then, I was

concentrating on the castle and not looking at him. I was afraid my blush would give me away if I looked at his face.

"There," he said softly, releasing my hand. "All done."

The ache didn't leave my core. In fact, with the removal of his hand, it grew stronger. I wanted him to touch me again. I *needed* him to touch me again.

Noah leaned back, examining his work. The castle was almost finished. It wasn't elaborate or immense, but it was beautiful with clean lines and simple towers that reminded me of a princess's castle. It looked like something Sleeping Beauty would be glad to claim as her own.

"It's gorgeous," I said. Noah grinned.

"You have some sand on your cheek," Noah replied, reaching a hand out to wipe it away. His fingers were gentle and warm against my face as he gently brushed the tiny grains from my skin. I shivered slightly, the heat in my core growing again.

Noah didn't pull his hand away once the sand was gone. His eyes focused on mine, pulling me deep into the pools of blue that led straight to his soul. His fingers caressed the back of my neck, pulling me into him. I met him halfway, winding my arms around his neck. His mouth slanted over mine, joining us together as if we had always meant to be. The kiss stole the air from my lungs and filled my body with light. My chest tightened and burned with a need that wasn't just physical. I wanted to dive into him like an ocean.

His tongue found mine, sending a bolt of hunger through me that was so strong I wasn't sure I'd survive. He tasted better than I could have imagined. His fingers tangled in my hair, pulling me into him. He wanted me as badly as I wanted him.

The sand was coarse beneath my knees in a beautiful contrast to the silkiness of his lips. My body was afire with sensation but totally focused on his kiss. The sun was warm against my hair, the sand rough against my legs, the ocean sighing in pleasure, but all I cared about was the warmth of Noah's lips against mine. The way his hands pressed into my hair, drawing me nearer to him.

Noah's phone began to ring. It buzzed in his pocket like an angry hornet while making an annoying old-school telephone ring. One hand released my head and slipped into his pocket to silence the intruding sound. The phone was only quiet for a moment before returning to it's incessant noise.

Noah tipped his face away from mine reluctantly, releasing me so he could fumble in his pocket to make the phone stop. I struggled to breathe and regain my senses. His kiss was overwhelmingly good. He pressed the screen of his phone, grumbling under his breath before reaching for me again. I wanted to kiss him again, but as soon as his fingers touched my skin, the phone began to vibrate.

"I think someone wants your attention as much as I do," I whispered. The spell of the kiss was broken.

"It's just work. They don't seem to understand that I'm on vacation," he whispered back, stealing a kiss on my cheek. "If I don't answer them, they'll just keep calling. I have a feeling I need to go attend to some business. I'm sorry. It'll probably take a while."

"How do you have cell service out here? You must be good friends with Jack Saunders to afford those roaming fees," I said, the idea suddenly hitting me. Cell service for non-locals was ridiculously priced.

Noah waved his hand through the air. "It's not that bad."

I raised my eyebrows at him and cocked my head to the side. I knew those rates were outrageous. "You're not fooling anyone with that. 'Fess up. You're at least a little more successful than just a bartender to the billionaires."

Noah laughed, the corners of his eyes crinkling. "Maybe. Maybe stealing phone minutes is just one of my many talents." He smiled. His blue eyes sparkled at me and the corners of his lips begged to be kissed again. I leaned forward, wanting to kiss him again, but the phone buzzed just a second before our lips could touch.

"I think your phone is trying to defend your honor," I said, sitting back on my heels. Noah glanced at the screen but didn't answer it.

"Can I take you out to dinner tonight?" His question took me off guard. I was expecting a quip, not a date proposal. Besides, I had promised myself no more dating tourists.

"You already bought me breakfast..." I stalled. I wanted to see him again, but I didn't want my heart broken when he left.

"Yes. I guess I'm going about it backwards. It's usually dinner *then* breakfast." He gave me a naughty wink and I couldn't help but blush slightly at the innuendo. "So, dinner?"

I didn't want to date a tourist again. I knew we were going to have a great time, that I would love to be in his company- that I craved his company- but I didn't want to get attached. He was leaving. He wasn't permanent.

I looked up at him with every intention of saying no. Even after that mind-blowing kiss, *especially* after that kiss, I needed to stay away from him, or I was going to fall hard. But as I looked into his sky-blue eyes, his smile forced my mouth from the "no" shape to "yes" shape.

"Yes. All right. Dinner," I stuttered. He was just too damn cute to say no to.

Noah beamed. "Excellent! What would you like to eat?"

"You mean you didn't have that planned already?" I teased. He hit the quiet button on his phone again.

"Nope. Just knew that I wanted to see you again today. Dinner seemed like a good reason. Anything you want?" He focused those blue eyes on me again, and I felt my temperature rising. *Anything I wanted*? I wanted him.

"Anything I want, huh?" I thought for a moment, but my brain just wasn't on food. "I want your favorite food."

Noah's dark brows came together in a question. He ran a hand through his dark hair as he clarified, "My favorite food?"

"Yup." I nodded.

"What if my favorite food is anchovy pizza with mustard sauce?"

"Then I will be eating pizza crusts for dinner tonight." I gave him an impish grin.

"You know I'm half-tempted to do that now, right?" Noah's blue eyes sparkled with mischief.

"Please don't! That actually sounds terrible, and I would like to eat tonight." I put my hand on his and my heart jumped in my chest.

"Okay," Noah said with a grin. "How does seven sound?"

"Works for me," I replied, going over my schedule in my head. No other plans for tonight, and Brooke would be busy with tagging her sharks.

"Where can I pick you up?" he asked, silencing his phone again.

"How about the parking lot of Adele's?"

"What? You don't want to give me your home address? Are you afraid I might be a serial killer?" Noah narrowed his eyes as though he were serious, but his voice told me he was still playing.

"No, I don't want to give my roommates a reason to point and laugh." I remembered the last tourist I had pick me up. The wolf whistles from the boys had followed us out into the street, and that was after Brooke had questioned his motives and made sure he had appropriate protection.

"So, you're embarrassed by me?" Noah gave a pretend pout.

"No!" I exclaimed and then took a breath. "I'm embarrassed of wolf whistles and embarrassing stories. My coworkers are like family and they think it's funny whenever I go out on a date. It took them two weeks of teasing before they realized that I was actually working at the bar and not just getting dressed up for fun."

"They sound charming," he said with a laugh.

"I love them, but they've decided that I'm their innocent little sister. They like to tease, but they're also very protective of me. They're like the older brothers I never had." I shook my head and smiled. "I'm really just saving you from interrogation."

"I don't know, I could go for some embarrassing stories of you," Noah said thoughtfully.

I punched his arm. "You have to earn those stories. I don't let just anyone hear them anymore."

"They must be good." Noah shot me a wolfish grin, and I could feel the blush heating my cheeks. Luckily, the buzz of his phone saved me. "They're starting to get desperate."

He hit "silence" once more and then brushed a strand of hair from my cheek and back behind my ear. In a graceful motion, he leaned forward, letting his lips graze the tender patch of skin at my temple in a gentle kiss. "I'll see you at seven."

I nodded, flood of want coursing though my stomach and stealing my words. Noah somehow had the ability to remove any coherent thought in my head and send my insides tumbling in the most pleasant way. I found myself wishing it was already dinnertime.

Noah stood and brushed the sand from his board shorts before giving me one last grin. If I hadn't been sitting, my knees would have gone weak at his smile. I waved as he turned, finally answering the phone with a curt greeting.

I watched him walk down the beach, checking out his perfect ass the entire way. In addition to being tall, dark, and handsome with eyes that could make a harpy melt, he also had a fantastic ass. He was as close to perfect as I could imagine.

I turned back to the sandcastle and put the last finishing touches on it. A few shells, some seaweed pennants, and finished digging the rest of the moat. I snapped a picture of it on my camera, wanting to save this sandcastle forever. It was perfect.

The waves were starting to creep up the beach with high tide. I dug the moat a little deeper to try and fend off the approaching waves, but I knew sandcastles were temporary. That was part of the beauty of them. They were only there for a short amount of time.

I stood and walked away, heading home. I didn't want to see the waves destroy our work. I knew that the sandcastle was the perfect metaphor for whatever was going on between Noah and me. Beautiful and amazing, but destined to fall apart. He was a tourist, and tourists leave. That's just what they do.

CHAPTER 8

I set the curling iron down and checked my handiwork. Beautiful, bouncing ringlets graced my head, but I knew that the second I stepped out into the tropical air they would go flat. I shook my head slowly at myself in the mirror. Even though I knew it was going to be straight by the time I got to the parking lot, I had gone to the trouble. Noah just had that effect on me. I wanted to look good for him.

"Oh, pretty," Brooke said, poking her head in the bathroom door. We shared the small bathroom and technically the curling iron was hers, but with the tropical humidity she had stopped trying to curl her hair after the second day. "So, who's the date with?"

"What makes you think I have a date?" I asked, glaring at her in the mirror.

She shot me a cheesy know-it-all smirk "Because you don't curl your hair for bartending gigs." Her smile widened. "And because you have been humming a Disney princess theme song for the past thirty minutes."

I scowled at her and she laughed. I put my makeup box

carefully away before turning to face her. "Don't tell anyone, okay? I don't need Lucas giving me a hard time again."

Brooke laughed and stepped out of the door to let me back into our shared bedroom. She ran and jumped onto her twin bed in the corner, tucking her legs under her once she landed. One of her tabloid magazines slid off the bed and landed on the floor, but she just ignored it.

"Your secret's safe with me." She held up her hand as though she were swearing in at a courtroom before a grin covered her face. "Now, who's the guy? Local or tourist?"

I went to the closet and pulled out my favorite light blue sundress. It was strapless and had a lacy bottom that made my legs look longer than they were. Brooke, with her amazing fashion sense, had picked it out for me at one of the tourist clothing shops. I loved it. It was the perfect dress to wear on my date.

"Well, you know what Lucas likes to call me..." I told Brooke as I carefully slid the dress over my head and dropped the bath towel.

Brooke squealed with delight and clapped her hands like an excited child. "Oooh, a tourist then!"

I rolled my eyes at her once they cleared the dress.

"Are you sure that's such a good idea? I mean, after the last one..." Brooke's smile faded, replaced by concern. "I just don't want to see you get hurt again."

I sat down into the small desk chair next to my bed and looked at her. "I don't know what I'm doing. I don't want to get burned again, but he makes my insides go all mushy just looking at him."

Brooke nodded thoughtfully before moving from the bed to stand behind me. She began to mess with my hair, pulling it up and away from my face.

"Then don't get burned," she said, as if it were the easiest thing in the world. "Know that you're walking into the fire, so wear your protective gear," she said. I turned and raised my eyebrows at her and she giggled. "That came out way dirtier than I had intended." Brooke placed a clip in my hair to keep it out of my eyes. "But what I mean is, go enjoy your date. But don't get attached. Know that this is just for fun. You are the one leaving him at the end of this, okay? Not the other way around."

"You don't think I'm an idiot then?" I asked her quietly as she finished messing with my hair.

She stepped forward so that she could look me straight in the eye. "No. You just love too easily." She smiled to soften her words. "Besides, have you seen the men I've dated?"

I giggled. Brooke went through boyfriends like water went through a sieve.

"Listen," she said, kneeling in front of my chair. "If he makes your insides mushy, then he's got to be good-looking. If he's a tourist on this island, then he's got to be rich. Good looking and rich? Enjoy him. Just make sure you have a little fire jacket around your heart this time."

"Fire jacket?" I asked.

"You know what I mean," she laughed, rolling her eyes. "Though the other kind is good to have too."

"So, don't fall in love with him. Just enjoy his company," I summarized and Brooke nodded. I picked up my purse and put on my cute heels.

"There is a third part to this as well," she said, her eyes dancing.

"What?" I racked my brain trying to think of what else she could add on that would be better than a 'little fire jacket.'

"You have to tell me all about it later."

I laughed and headed out to meet Noah.

THE SUN WAS warm on my shoulders as I waited patiently at the entrance to Dominic's Bar and Adele's Restaurant. The sun was just beginning it's descent but hadn't yet transitioned into the golds and shadows of sunset. I watched the normal parade of beat-up cars pull in and out of the parking lot while I waited for Noah to arrive.

Two local boys waved to me as they walked into Adele's with their mom, and an obvious tourist couple snapped photographs in front of the giant dolphin sculpture in front of Dominic's Bar. The woman with the khaki shorts I had seen earlier stomped into the bar with a scowl on her face. I had a feeling she was getting a drink to soothe a rough day, and after wading around in the mangroves without proper shoes, I would want a drink too.

I glanced at my watch to see the digital numbers flip to seven. I bit my lip and glanced around, but I didn't see him anywhere. My dress ruffled slightly in the tropical breeze. I hoped he wasn't going to stand me up. On the other hand, though, if he stood me up I wouldn't have to deal with the problem of dating a tourist. He would just be another jerk who'd blown me off.

Only he wasn't a jerk. I knew that. He was handsome and funny, and had a sweetness that I couldn't explain. He made my world seem brighter than it was before. My hand drifted up to my lips, my fingers touching my face where he had kissed me. I wanted to kiss him again.

"Don't fall for him," I whispered softly to myself. "He's just a tourist. Don't get in too deep..."

"Too deep with what?" A strong masculine voice asked, surprising me.

I yelped and spun around to see Noah leaning up

against the building. I wondered just how long he had been standing there watching me with that crooked grin. He took my breath away. The sun glinted off his dark hair, and his blue eyes matched the sky. A crooked half-smile made his face somehow more handsome. In a nice, light blue polo shirt and expensive-looking tan shorts, he looked good enough to eat. I hoped for a second he was what was for dinner.

"Nothing," I said, hoping I wasn't blushing too badly. "Just talking to myself."

He straightened from the wall and offered me his arm like I was royalty. "You look beautiful, Izzy."

I blushed as I took his arm in mine, feeling the warmth of his skin under my fingers. His muscles flexed slightly as I touched him, sending a thrill up my fingers and down my spine.

"What are we having for dinner tonight?" I asked. I realized I didn't actually care. I would have been happy to eat sand if it meant that I got to sit at the same table as Noah. I would have eaten it with a smile on my face.

"It's a surprise," he answered, leading me back behind the bar and down a path that ran along the beach. I rarely used the path because it ran down to the beach houses, which would make sense why Noah had used it instead of driving to the restaurant. He was staying at one of those beach houses.

"Are we going to the house where the party was?" I asked as he guided me along the path.

"Yes," he answered. I faltered slightly in my step, remembering all the people at the party. At least some of them must be staying at the giant home. I was hoping for a slightly more romantic dinner than that.

"Don't worry." Noah must have felt my hesitance. He put

his hand gently over mine, his voice soft and low. "I'm renting a little bungalow on the property. We aren't actually going to the house."

"Oh, so you're taking me to your place then?" I batted my eyelashes up at him. "Maybe I *should* have made you run the coworker gauntlet."

The path ran through a grove of banyan trees. I had always liked this part of the path because it reminded me of being in a big tree fort. The brown, woody limbs tangled above us, creating a sky of green. The sunlight flickered through the gaps, dappling the ground and casting warm shadows across our bodies.

"My intentions are mostly honorable." He winked.

"Mostly?"

"Well, there might be some things I would like to do with you that an older brother wouldn't necessarily appreciate." Noah's eyes caught mine, their blue depths holding a dark warmth that sent shivers of desire all the way to my toes. "But I can guarantee, you'd enjoy it."

I let out a slight gasp of want. The idea of doing things that my 'older brothers' wouldn't approve of stirred the coals deep in my belly. I wanted to kiss him again right there, and possibly just take him in the trees to be my own.

"Shit," he murmured, making me frown. With a strong tug, he pulled me off the path and behind a tree.

"What are you doing?" I gasped, but my words were muffled by his hand as he concealed us from the path. I fought him slightly, but his grip was sure and strong. It would take a good fight to break free, and I wasn't sure what was going on yet. Through the tree branches I could just make out the path. I tried to see what was going on, but I was too distracted by the feel of his body pressed against mine. He was solid and warm on my back. Despite my best efforts, my body was melting into his. His arms were wrapped tightly around me, his scent enveloping me with its deliciousness.

He held a finger to his lips, asking me silently to be quiet. I nodded and he released me, but kept me pressed against him with his arm. I wondered if he could feel my heart pounding out of my chest. I could escape him now if I wanted, but I was glued to his body as if he had me tied to him with ropes.

The woman with the khaki shorts came down the path. I was beginning to think she was following me since she kept showing up wherever I happened to be. The angry look plastered on her face told me that I did not want to run into her.

"I swear I saw them come this way," she muttered under her breath as she passed in front of our tree. I held my breath, afraid that she might hear it and find us. She continued on down the path, her mumbling growing quieter with every step.

We waited for a long time, silently pressed against one another until he was sure we were safe. Thoughts ran through my mind. Why was he hiding? Who was that woman? And of course, my mind went to the darkest places it could while we waited. *Maybe he's a wanted criminal and she's a bounty hunter. It's his wife. It's his boss. He owes her money. She was his last girlfriend and she followed him here and she'll kill me out of jealousy.* Each thought was more absurd than the last, but in the quiet of my mind, my imagination ran wild.

The sun began to touch the horizon, deepening the shadows of the branches. Noah stepped onto the path, motioning me to stay put while he checked it out. He took a few steps and then smiled and waved me back to the path.

"I think she's gone. The path loops around past the house, but she shouldn't have a reason to turn around." He reached out his hand for me.

"Who was she?" I didn't immediately take his hand. "Why were you hiding from her?"

Noah ran his outstretched hand through his dark hair, the muscles in his arm stretching the fabric of his shirt. "Danica Lewis. She's a reporter."

"A reporter?" That possibility had not been one of the billions running through my mind as we hid behind the tree.

"Yeah." He sighed and took a step toward me, his eyes honest as he spoke. "My company just went through a big lawsuit. We won, but we weren't popular because of it. She wants an interview. I think she believes that a scathing interview with the 'Devil of Real Estate' will jump-start her career. I told her no. I have no idea how she followed me here."

"They call you 'The Devil of Real Estate?'"

He gave me a small smile. "Figuratively speaking."

I nodded, and he reached for my hand. I let him take it, his large hands wrapping my smaller ones with his warmth. I loved the way his hands felt.

"I'm sorry if I scared you." His thumbs caressed the back of my hand. "I just don't want my vacation ruined by an over-eager reporter. She's not exactly a nice person."

"Have you interviewed with her before?" I asked. Noah tucked my arm into his elbow, starting us down the path again. The setting sun glimmered through the tree branches and made the world into gold and silver shadows. We walked slowly, not wanting to risk catching up to her.

"She covered the lawsuit." The corners of his mouth went down in disgust. "I dreaded walking past her every morning because she had the most bitter things to say to try and get a good soundbite."

"She sounds like a lovely human being," I cracked. Noah snorted and gave me a small squeeze. "You know, this does tell me that you actually are successful and not just good at stealing cell phone minutes."

"I was afraid you might come to that conclusion, but why do you think that?" Noah asked, his eyes on the path.

"One, reporters don't hound unimportant people. Two, you have multiple billionaire friends. And then three, the fact that you have a functioning phone on an island in the middle of the ocean." I ticked off the reasons on my fingers.

"All right," he said slowly. "I might be a *little* important."

"You aren't going to tell me, are you?" I asked. He shook his head. "Well, then I'll try and figure it out. What was the lawsuit about?"

Noah stopped in his tracks and turned to face me. "You really don't know? It was all over CNN for a good week."

I shook my head from side to side. "I don't have much time for TV, and we don't have cable at the research facility. If it isn't about an approaching hurricane, then I don't follow it."

A soft, slow smile came over Noah's face. His eyes danced as his smile grew. "Well, isn't that something..."

"So, are you going to tell me, or what?" I asked impatiently. His smile just grew wider.

"If you don't know, I'd rather not tell you. It wasn't a pleasant experience, and it's really nice to talk with someone without constantly being reminded of your failures."

I thought about that for a moment as we started walking again. I thought about my own failures and how much it would suck to have a reporter hounding me for more.

Having some of them reported in the local newspaper when I was a kid had been bad enough, but the idea of having them broadcast to the world was terrible.

"I understand." I gave him a squeeze and leaned into his strong arm. "Failures suck. I know they're supposed to teach you some sort of lesson, and that it can work out for the better, but they still suck. They leave a bitter taste in your mouth. I guess that makes success that much sweeter, but *ugh*."

Noah chuckled at my disgusted noise. "Between the lawsuit and the wedding, I've had enough failures."

My heart sunk to my toes and threatened to continue on down through China. *Wedding?* My brain rebelled against the word. *He's married. He's been leading me on this whole time. I kissed a married man.* A panic went through me and I dropped his arm and pushed him away. No wonder he was so charming. He had a wife to practice all his lines on first.

"What do you mean, 'wedding?'" I asked coldly.

Noah's shoulders slumped, and his face fell. The shadows of the trees crossed his features, darkening them. He put his hands in his pockets and kicked at the ground, his eyes following a small stone on the path.

"I forgot you don't know about that either." He looked up at me, his eyes full of hurt and his brow pinched to almost pain. "I was recently left at the altar."

"So you're not married?" I mentally slapped myself for being tactless as relief flooded my voice. I wasn't the other woman after all.

Noah gave a bitter chuckle and kicked the stone again, sending it spinning into the roots of a tree. "Nope. She didn't even bother going to the church. She came from a big society family, so it was supposed to be the social event of the year. Even the mayor was there. She made one of her poor bridesmaids walk up the aisle and tell me she wasn't going through with it. In front of the whole congregation." A spiteful smile danced briefly across his face. "I don't think they're friends anymore."

My hands went to my mouth in shock. I'd always thought that kind of thing only happened in movies. "That's terrible! I'm so sorry!"

He shrugged, obviously trying to pretend that he didn't care despite the pain etched all over his face. Whoever she was, she had hurt him. I was halfway surprised he was even willing to talk to another female again.

"I really thought she was the one." He looked up, his eyes full of unshed tears. "You know, growing old together and spending cold nights cuddled up next to the fireplace kind of thing. I was wrong. I didn't see it coming."

I took another step forward. We were almost touching again. "I'm so sorry. I can't imagine doing that to someone. Did she give you a reason?" As soon as the words were out of my mouth, I grimaced a little. Tact was just not with me today.

"Money." He spat the word out like it was a vile, bitter thing. "I found that out later. She learned that I had turned down a job with Jack's father. It wasn't what I wanted to do and I had bigger and better plans, but she didn't believe in me. She just wanted the paycheck."

"I'm sorry," I said quietly. He looked up and over at a tree branch above my head.

"She ended up marrying some banker. They divorced as soon as he went bankrupt." The corners of his mouth turned up in a bitter smile, but his eyes stayed cold.

I wasn't sure quite how to respond to that. Another 'sorry' just didn't seem adequate. 'Good job dodging *that* bullet!' didn't seem quite appropriate either, so I just stayed silent.

Noah's eyes returned from the branch to my face. The last few rays of golden sunlight caught the angles of his face, making him look older and more stern. I liked the carefree and happy Noah better.

"It was one of those failures that turns out to be a good thing in the end," he said quietly. "But the fact that it was such a disaster still stings. It's on my Wikipedia page now. I'm the 'left-at-the-altar guy.'" He found another rock to kick, sending it hurtling down the path. I took his arm and pressed my cheek into his shoulder.

"And here I thought it was bad being the 'always-falls-for-tourists girl,'" I said without thinking. I cringed a little once the words were out, but I started walking, hoping that he wouldn't catch it.

"The 'always-falls-for-tourists girl?'" He turned and grinned at me, and I could feel the blush heat my cheeks.

"It's just a nickname," I said lamely. "Not interesting at all."

"Oh no, it's very interesting," he insisted. "Besides, I just told you my dirty laundry."

I fidgeted for a moment, wishing I could devise a way out of telling him. It wasn't so much that it was a horrible thing, just more embarrassing than anything else. Especially when I had to tell it to a tourist I was interested in. I looked over at him, and he just raised his dark eyebrows, waiting.

"Fine," I sighed. "The majority of eligible men on the island are tourists, so the past few guys I 'dated' weren't exactly locals," I explained. "Anyway, the last one promised me the moon and the stars. I believed him and told everyone I was going to go back to the mainland with him."

"And he didn't take you with him?"

"Worse. He was actually here for his bachelor party. I was his last hurrah," I said, sickened at how gullible I had been. "It was all a lie." I looked down, feeling the insecurity and shame bubble up again. "I had told everyone. I had practically bought my plane ticket."

My voice faltered at the end. I didn't want to tell Noah how the jerk had laughed at me. How I had trudged through the town and everyone had shot me pitying looks. The shame of everyone finding out that I had been duped and dumped. The well-meaning but awkward questions from my mainland friends asking when I was going to come visit them. My mom's reaction. I cleared my throat and tossed my hair behind my shoulder. I was stronger now.

"But I learned my lesson. No more tourists."

Noah faced me, his hands on my shoulders. The heat of his palms against my bare skin set my body afire with want. I wasn't sure if he was trembling or if I was, but either way my body was humming. Ice blue eyes held me in their thrall. They were full of kindness and attraction, and it was intoxicating.

"What about me? I'm a tourist." His voice was deep and playful. I stared at his perfect lips, wanting to kiss them, as they formed the words.

"Yeah, well, I never said I was a good student."

The fingers of one of Noah's hands made their way to my chin, moving me into a gentle, yet insistent kiss. The kiss deepened, my lips parting to give him more. His kiss was hot and deep, banishing every unhappy thought from my mind. He tucked his head, breaking the connection and allowing me to replenish the much needed oxygen for my aching body. I took an unsteady breath, keeping my eyes closed, feeling lightheaded and wonderful.

At least this time I know what's coming, I thought to myself.

I know this is just for now and not forever. I can enjoy this now, or I can regret never having it. I opened my eyes to see his blue ones. *I choose to enjoy it.*

"You are so beautiful," Noah whispered. His smile was soft and full of affection. Butterflies danced in my stomach.

"Thanks," I whispered. My voice didn't seem to work anymore. I cleared my throat, trying to steady myself by holding onto him. I wasn't sure if that was working, but I wasn't about to let go. Being dizzy in his arms was far better than walking straight alone. "So, what about that dinner I was promised?"

Noah laughed, the rich sound filling the tunnel of trees. The sun had set, turning the branches into a dark mystery of shadows and secrets. I could see the lights of houses ahead on the path, urging us on to civilization. Noah took my hand in his, pulling me forward as we went to eat the dinner he had planned.

he sound of Noah's feet changed as he stepped from the path onto a smaller, sand-packed one that led toward the rear of Owen's beach home. The sky was fading from lilac to navy as the stars came out to play with the ocean. He led me past some palm trees to an adorable bungalow on the beach.

It was right on the water with the back porch suspended over the ocean on piers that dove into the sea at high tide. Big windows were open to the night air, and I could already smell the scent of food wafting out of them. The front door was flanked by two palm trees leading up to a wooden porch that wrapped around the entire house.

Noah hurried to open the front door, holding it for me like a true gentleman. The inside was just as charming as the outside. Teak floors and comfortable furniture filled the small space with blue and green accents everywhere. It felt like a home instead of a beach house.

The little bungalow appeared to be a main room, kitchen, and then a bedroom with an en suite bath. Set up in the main living area was a round wooden table with candles, two big white plates, and glasses. A smaller rectangular table stood beside it with buffet style warming dishes and carafes of milk and orange juice.

"M'lady," Noah said with a smile as he pulled out a chair for me to sit. I sat as delicately as I could, and while I got comfortable he lit the two candles. Warm light flickered through the cozy room and added a romantic vibe.

With a flair, he opened the four lids of food on the serving table. Inside each warmer was a breakfast food. Steam from bacon, hash browns, pancakes, and scrambled eggs with cheese and peppers filled the room and made my mouth water.

I clapped my hands with delight. "This looks fantastic!"

Noah let out a little sigh of relief and grinned. "I was hoping you would like it. You said to make my favorite, so here it is."

"I love breakfast food. It really should just be anytime meal food because it's so good." I handed him my plate, and he began scooping food in neat portions onto it. "This is so much better than anchovy pizza with mustard sauce."

"There's maple syrup, ketchup and hot sauce if you want it," he said nodding toward the end of the table. It looked like it was real maple syrup. The man certainly knew how to do breakfast right.

He handed the plate back to me, and I had a hard time waiting to eat while he quickly filled his own plate with the delicious breakfast food. I poured a little maple syrup on the plate and tasted it on my finger. It was the real stuff. The expensive stuff. The stuff my mom only got us on Christmas. I nearly poured the rest of the bottle on my pancakes.

Once he sat down, he grinned. "Let's eat!"

The pancakes were possibly the best pancakes I had ever had in my life, and I've had a lot of pancakes. They were light and fluffy, but had enough weight to them that they didn't feel flat or too little. They were buttery and delicious. Combined with the maple syrup, I could have lived on that alone for a year.

"So does this count as you making me breakfast, or dinner?" I asked, reaching for the ketchup. The hash browns were crispy and perfect, and the eggs melted in my mouth with little explosions of heat from the peppers. I was fairly sure I had died and gone to food heaven.

"Whichever you want it to be," he said as he poured maple syrup over all the contents on his plate. "I'll even make you dinner in the morning if you want."

I giggled at his joke. Noah took his fork and mixed all the contents of his plate into a pile, stirring in the maple syrup. I made a snorting noise at his culinary decision.

"What?" he asked, his mouth full of maple syrup breakfast goodness.

"You eat like my little brother," I explained, pointing to his plate with my fork. "He likes it all mixed together too."

"I like the way all the tastes combine..." Big blue eyes looked at me in complete innocence, thinking I was making fun of him.

I smiled. "That's what he says, too!"

Noah swallowed and grinned. "So you have a little brother? Is he here on the island with you?"

I shook my head. "No, he's back in the States. He starts high school this year. Will you hand me the orange juice?"

Noah's eyebrows rose, but he reached for the juice. "High school?" I could see his brain trying to do mental math to figure out if I was far younger than I looked.

"Thanks," I said as I took the juice and poured a big glass. "The two of us are nine years apart."

"Oh," he replied, a relieved smile lit up his face. He put

another bite of food on his fork and got ready to put it in his mouth. "Are you two close?"

I shook my head. "Not really. I got stuck watching him a lot growing up, but now that we're so far apart, I kind of miss him. He's a good kid."

"Absence makes the heart grow fonder." Noah took another bite.

"Or forgetful. Though I doubt I'll forget all the frogs he put in my pillowcase anytime soon. Little child was a brat." I laughed. It was a funny memory now, but at the time I nearly took him to the local pond and drowned him. "Do you have any siblings?"

Noah swallowed. "An older brother."

"What does he do?" I added some more maple syrup to my plate. It was just too good.

"He works for me," Noah said with a grin. I set my fork down and eyed him.

"See? I knew you had to be successful. Reporters, Jack Saunders, and an older brother that works for you. You must do more than just flip distressed properties. What do you do?"

Noah shook his head. "Not telling."

"Why?" I took another bite and swallowed. "Do you work for the mob?"

Noah laughed, nearly choking on his eggs. "No, no mob. I've been accused of it, but I can honestly say that I don't work for the mob."

"Hmm. Do I need to be worried about what you do? I mean, if you're a hit man, I'd like to know." I felt a little bit of anxiety at the fact that he didn't want to tell me exactly what he did for a living. I was getting the very clear impression that he had a good deal of wealth, but there were a lot of shady ways to make money. I wasn't nearly as afraid as I should have been, though. For some reason, every fiber of my being already trusted him completely. Even the little worrywart fibers that liked to whisper things in the wee hours and didn't fully trust that gravity existed, trusted him.

"You only need to worry if you're a distressed property," he answered, leaning back in his chair and pushing his empty plate forward.

I patted my chest. "Nope, still a human." I played with my fork in the last remnants of egg on my plate.

"I'll tell you this," he said, relenting slightly. "I have several businesses, and they all deal with real estate in some form. I am very successful with what I do. And the reason I don't want to tell you, is because I'm afraid you'll be tempted to go Google it and you'll find out about those failures I was telling you about earlier. The press hasn't been very nice to me, and there are a lot of lies being spread around."

I set my fork down. "So why don't you just tell me now? Then I'll know the truth."

He sighed and ran a hand through his hair. "If I tell you, I'm afraid you won't look at me like you are right now. I'm afraid you'll look at me the way everyone else does, and that would kill me."

His eyes focused on mine, the candlelight flickering and bringing out the handsomeness of his face. There was an energy to him that I couldn't escape. Didn't want to escape. At that moment, I didn't care what he did. I just wanted to be with him. Besides, it didn't matter what he did anyway. He was leaving soon.

"You haven't asked me when I'm leaving yet," Noah remarked as if he could read my mind. For all I knew, he could.

"Maybe I don't want to know. Maybe I like the illusion that you might stay." I swallowed hard. I hadn't realized that the words were true until I spoke them. The idea of him staying was like being told I could have the moon. I wanted it so badly, but I knew realistically it wasn't going to happen.

"How about this, then? I'll tell you what I do when I leave."

I thought about it for a moment. That was an acceptable answer. He could keep his secret, I could keep looking at him as though he walked on water, and when he left, both our illusions would be shattered, but in private. "Then I hope I never find out."

I looked into his eyes and I wished that there wasn't a table separating us. I wanted to kiss him so badly. His refusal to disclose his job to me only added an air of mystery that I couldn't get enough of.

Noah's eyes reflected the candlelight.

"Did you know that my back porch has the best view on the island?" he asked quietly. I smiled. The man knew how to change a subject.

"Is that so?"

"Best view on the island." He crossed his arms with a smug smile.

"And you've been everywhere on the island to check this?"

Noah grinned, standing up and offering me his hand. I couldn't refuse the opportunity to touch him, so I took it and followed him out onto the back porch. He only let me go so that he could close the door behind us.

I leaned up against the railing, looking up at the moon. Her silver light reflected down on the ocean waves, turning their white tips bright. The sky was dark purple now, and the air was humid, dark, and full of promise.

"Yup, definitely the best view on the island," Noah whispered, making me turn. He wasn't looking at the night sky or the ocean. He was looking at me. It was slightly cheesy, but I enjoyed the compliment.

Noah moved forward, gathering me up in his arms. The masculine scent of his light cologne was exhilarating. His mouth slowly slanted to mine, sending small thrills up and down my spine. He went further, tasting me with his tongue like I was something to be savored. A low moan escaped my lips as he pulled me closer to him, his arms strong and demanding around me. His kiss was sweeter than heaven and hotter than hell.

I didn't want to fall for another tourist. *You're not falling*, I told myself. *You're simply enjoying.* I knew he was going to leave and I would be sad. But I would also be far more disappointed if I missed this. His kiss was insistent, intoxicating, and driving me insane. I wanted to melt into him and let him melt into me. I wanted to kiss every inch of his skin. *Every* inch.

I had never been so turned on by a kiss before. It was as if Noah knew everything I loved in a kiss and was delivering and then some. I had never felt this sort of connection with another human being before. I didn't want to get hurt, but I wasn't going to miss this either. *Just one last tourist...*

As if he could read my thoughts, he began to press into me more, leading me back toward the door of the house. I smiled as I walked backward, hoping that I wouldn't trip over a loose board on the deck.

CHAPTER 10

I, of course, did trip. But Noah was there to catch me. His strong arms wrapped around my waist, and he pushed me up against the wall of the house. I was pinned by his arms, and I had no intention of escaping. With slow, sensual lips, he nibbled down my jaw, kissing my throat as he made his way down to my collarbone. Each touch was erotic and hot. My body was responding with pure want and arching into him without me telling it to.

A soft breeze came across from the ocean, cooling the hot kisses on my skin. I wondered if people could see us, since we were still outside and not secluded by windows or walls. Noah's hand was planted firmly on my breast, his fingers massaging me through the fabric of my dress. I moaned quietly, realizing that the only people who could see us at this private villa would be boats out on the ocean. With the darkening night, that would be close to impossible, but the thrill of possibly being seen was still there.

Noah's hand slid down my side to the hem of my dress, tracing the lacy edge against my thigh. The light touch on the sensitive skin sent shivers up my spine. He chuckled, the sound reverberating deep in his chest as he slid his leg between mine. It was strong and steady, and I rocked against it. His hands went back up to the collar of my dress. With a feather-light touch, he grazed the skin right above the collar of my strapless dress. I sucked in a breath as he suddenly pulled down on the fabric, exposing both breasts to the night air.

"Mmm," he hummed into my skin as he bent his head to take one in his mouth. I didn't bother to repress my moaning, making him smile against my skin. His five-o'clock shadow was rough against my soft skin, but I loved it. I loved when he touched me. I couldn't believe I was ready for this step in our relationship so fast, but I wanted him.

My hands tangled in his dark hair as his mouth worked magic. His tongue caressed and teased, pebbling my nipple into a tight ball which he bit gently with his teeth. A high-pitched thrum vibrated through my entire body as I ground against his thigh with my pelvis. My head fell back against the house, and my hips pressed into him with my back arched to give him the best access I could. I wanted him to take all of me. I felt his smile against my damp skin as he went to the other breast to continue his exquisite torture.

He shifted his weight, removing the thigh that was perilously close to getting me off and putting his hands on my waist. With a spin, he picked me up and set me on the thick balcony. He made sure I had my balance so that my arm wrapped around the support beam. Despite the width of the balcony rail, I was still afraid I might fall. It was higher than I was really comfortable with, and I wasn't sure just how deep the ocean was below, even at high tide.

"Don't let me fall," I whispered, a little anxious as to what he had planned.

He responded with a kiss, wrapping one arm around my

waist so that he pinned me to the support beam. His kisses moved down to the sensitive area just below my ear where my shoulder and neck joined. "I've got you."

His free hand slid up my thigh, reminding me that I was wearing a dress and that my knees were splayed open. His hand didn't stop at the hem of my dress; instead, he continued up my inner thigh and sent heat surging through my core. His fingers caressed the lace of the little panties I had chosen. They were light blue like the dress and more lace and string than fabric.

"Pretty," he murmured into my shoulder, moving his lips to nibble on my collarbone. The pad of his thumb stroked me through the lace, and I moaned. I wanted him so badly that I couldn't think straight. His clever fingers danced under the thin lace and touched bare skin.

I knew I was already wet and ready. He made a happy, masculine noise into my shoulder as he began to pleasure me with his fingers. His thumb kept a steady pulse against my pleasure center while slowly working one finger, and then two into my ready body.

It was pure heaven. My breaths were coming quick and fast, my hands gripping the support beam more and more tightly. I was losing myself completely to his magic touch. My body twitched, pausing on the edge of beautiful oblivion. I had never gotten to this point of orgasm so quickly.

"I've got you," he whispered again, tightening his grip on my waist. He held me safe above the waves as I lost my body to sheer ecstasy. The sound of the water roared in my ears, or maybe it was just my own heartbeat, but I clung to Noah and let myself be washed away.

I whimpered as my mind slowly returned, little aftershocks of pleasure still shaking my limbs.

"Bed. Now." I couldn't make a coherent sentence, but I

needed to have him inside of me. That instant. I was thinking of simply jumping off the rail and jumping his bones right there on the porch.

Without a moment's hesitation, he picked me up and threw me over his shoulder in a fireman's carry. I was glad, because I was pretty sure my knees were made of jelly. Plus, I liked the idea of him carrying me off to bed like a caveman.

He tossed me onto the bed, and I grinned as I bounced. I rose to my knees and wiggled out of my dress, tossing it to the side. His eyes went wide and dark as he looked me over, and judging by the stress on his zipper, he enjoyed it.

I watched in fascination as he pulled his polo over his head in a smooth movement. The room was dark except for the moonlight shining through the window. His muscles caught the light, making him gleam like the men in my best wet dreams.

He fished in his pocket for a moment to pull out his wallet. He opened it and pulled out a cellophane square. I held open my hands and he tossed it to me so he could unbuckle his shorts and step out of them. With my eyes on him, I carefully opened the package. I could see just how excited he was by the massive tent in his boxers. My lady parts tingled with excitement at what he was about to offer. I licked my lips, wanting to have him that second.

I slid to the floor, going to my knees before him. "Let me," I purred. He gave a slow nod as I reached for his boxers and pulled down. A little gasp of desire escaped me as he sprung free. He was utter male perfection, and he was about to be mine.

With seductive slowness, I kissed the velvet tip of his erection, stroking his delectable length with the lightest touch of my fingers. I gave him one slow lick with my tongue from stem to stern, watching the muscles in his abs tighten.

"Holy shit, Izzy," he growled, his voice rough with need. I grinned up at him through my eyelashes, letting him know exactly what my mouth could do. His hands tangled in my hair as his eyes rolled back in his head. Small, pleasure-filled sounds echoed through the room as I tasted him.

I pulled back, giving him one last kiss before sliding the condom down his engorged length. My body tightened with every inch I lowered. I wanted to envelope him like that.

He took my hands to help me stand, our eyes meeting. The blue of Noah's eyes went dark with storm clouds of want. Just his look had my body humming. His eyes left mine to travel up and down my body, and his mouth opened in awe.

"You are so beautiful," he whispered, wrapping his strong hand around my neck and pulling me into his kiss. His hot length pressed into my hip, his kiss hot and insistent. Together we stumbled back onto the bed.

His body pressed against mine as he pushed my panties to the side and positioned himself at my entrance. I arched my back, giving him full access. "Please..." I panted.

With terrible slowness, he slid into me an inch at a time until I was sure I could hold no more. He continued, pressing ever deeper. I cried out with pleasure; he felt even better than I had imagined in my dreams.

He pushed himself to the hilt, filling me completely and then held there. My world tightened around him as he began working himself back and forth with calm, even strokes. My hands went to his back, his ass, wanting to touch every wonderful inch of him.

"Noah..." I moaned. Even his name felt wonderful. I hooked my legs around his waist, my hands grabbing at the flexed muscles of his shoulders and arms. I wanted more of him, as much as I could handle and more, but he just kept his perfectly even pace. It was driving me wild.

I tightened my legs around him and twisted, rolling him under me so we switched positions and I was on top. He grinned and brushed a strand of hair from my face. I began to bounce, his hands going to my hips to match my tempo. I went fast and hard, letting my body take what it needed.

"Oh, fuck, Izzy," he groaned, letting his head fall back into the bed. His hips matched my cadence, our bodies meeting with a carnal sound that only added to my lust. He was everything I wanted. His body was heaven made of muscles and blue eyes.

His hands went wild, touching my hips, my stomach, my breasts, my ass, and my arms. It was like he wanted to touch me everywhere all at once. I understood the feeling as my hands used his pecs for balance. I needed more hands to touch him more.

He rose to his elbows, driving his full length deep into me. I gasped, meeting his eyes. His face was flushed. I loved that he was panting with want. His erratic breathing and the knowledge that it was I that was doing that to him turned me on like nothing I could imagine. I kept the undulating motion with my hips, watching his face contort with pleasure.

His thumb went to my nub again, still swollen and tender from his last touches. With the first brush, my temperature shot into the stratosphere. I was the one panting now, balanced on the edge of ecstasy.

Our eyes met, blue to green, and our worlds exploded. The look on his face sent me spiraling into oblivion. I tried to hold on, to hold back, but I was lost to his release. My body trembled against his, pulling him deeper inside of me. I never wanted to let him go.

After an infinite moment, I collapsed on his chest. We both were struggling for breath, our hearts nearly pounding out of our chests. He kissed me, his lips soft and gentle as I snuggled into the nook of his shoulder and wrapped a leg over his. I loved the way his heart was pounding.

"Stay the night," he whispered. It wasn't a question, but it wasn't a command either.

"I was hoping to," I replied, kissing the line of his pectoral muscle. "I'm not done with you yet."

He twitched against my leg, already growing hard.

"I knew breakfast really had been a good idea," he said quietly. I giggled and kissed him again. I had to agree. Breakfast was a great idea.

CHAPTER 11

Noah snored softly in his sleep beside me. I lay in bed for a few minutes, enjoying not only the luxury of sleeping in, but also waking up to a gorgeous naked man. Life was good.

The light on my phone blinked steadily, telling me that I had a new text message. The only problem was that it was across the room. Noah mumbled something and smushed his face into the pillow, and I had to work hard not to giggle. He was adorable when he slept.

With a silent smile, I slipped from the bed and walked on noiseless feet to the bathroom. The sheet shifted as I escaped its silky fingers, revealing Noah's perfect butt. I gave it an appreciative look before disappearing to find my clothes.

Part of the reason I loved my blue dress was that it didn't wrinkle. Wrinkle-free clothes make the "walk of shame" that much easier. I slid it over my head, feeling muscles stretch that I hadn't used in a while. I was sore in the most delightful of places, and the thought made me smile. Noah made me smile.

I grabbed my phone and stepped out to the back porch to check my messages and call my boss. Dr. Algos would be wondering where I was since it was past my usual check-in time.

The wood was cool under my feet as it was shaded from the morning sun, but the ocean was alive with sunlight. Every wave sparkled like it was made of diamonds as it danced ever closer to the shore, finally spilling onto the sand to reveal it's starry soul.

"Hey, Doc," I said after Dr. Algos picked up on the second ring.

"Did you have a nice time?" I could hear him walking along the dock toward the boats, a smile evident in his voice.

"Of course I did," I replied, trying to keep my voice innocent.

"When do we get to meet him?"

I groaned. "So Devon and Lucas can tease me about falling for another tourist? Not a chance."

Dr. Algos laughed gently. I didn't feel hurt when he teased me about my love life. I liked that he was interested enough to care, and yet he never said anything about my choices. He was the "cool dad" who let me make my own mistakes, but who was always there to help pick me up when I fell.

"I don't have much for you to do today. Since we're waiting on officially getting the Grove, I don't want to start anything new," Dr. Algos said. I could hear him putting something in the boat.

"Are you going on a dive later?" I asked.

"Yes. You and your new friend are welcome to join us, but I have a feeling you are going to turn me down." I could see his smile in my head. "If you could stop by later, though, and check the shark pups, then you can have the morning off."

"I will happily take the shark pups this afternoon." I grinned at the phone, even though I knew he couldn't see me. "Any update on the Grove?"

"Just the same goobelty-gook from the lawyers as last time. They keep telling me the sale should go through any day now. Don't worry about that today, though. Go enjoy your tourist."

I frowned slightly, but I knew he was right. Worrying about the Grove wasn't going to help anything. The sale would go through, and I could continue my research by next week. It would give me something to keep my mind off of Noah leaving.

As if thinking of Noah called him, I heard the thump of feet in the bedroom and the creak of a door.

"All right. I'll check the pups and see you later. Have fun on your dive," I said into the phone as a tousled and very sexy man opened the porch door. "Bye, Doc."

I clicked off the phone and Noah stepped onto the porch. He was wearing nothing but a pair of boxers. It was difficult not to stare.

"Good morning, sleepy head," I said with a smile. He stretched his hands overhead and the muscles in his chest and arms rippled under the morning sun. I swore my temperature went up five degrees just looking at him.

"Good morning, gorgeous," he murmured, leaning in to kiss my cheek before stretching again. It was a simple act of caring that made me feel a warm, pleasant glow all the way to my toes. He liked me. I had no idea why it was so important to me that he did, but I loved that he liked me.

"Did I wake you up?" I asked, holding up the phone. He shook his head.

"Nope. I'm usually up at the crack of dawn. This is the equivalent of me sleeping until noon. I haven't slept that well in ages."

"Must be the tropical air," I said coyly. He came to the balcony, putting a muscled arm on either side of me and leaning in close. My heart started beating faster, my body aching to feel him again.

"Must be." He pulled back, leaving me wanting more. "Can you play tourist with me today?"

"I would be happy to show you around the island," I started, but he shook his head, coming in close again. His legs pressed against mine, pushing me against the balcony.

"No. Pretend you're a tourist and come play with me."

"Okay." It was hard to think with him that close, with his body against mine. Coherent thoughts on scheduling the day were the last thing on my mind, but I managed to do it. "I just have to check on the pups this afternoon. You can come if you want."

"If it means I get to spend more time with you, then I'll go grocery shopping with you," he said, his voice low and masculine. I giggled at the idea of him walking behind me as I picked out eggs for the entire research team.

"Can I take you snorkeling?" I asked, looking up into his clear-blue eyes. I could play tourist. I would just play a very well-informed tourist.

"I was thinking margaritas on the beach, but I'll take snorkeling with a marine biologist." He gave me a serious face. "Just as long as there's no test at the end."

"Oh, I was going to make you name every species of nudibranch!" I teased.

"I'm not sure I want to even know what that is."

"They're basically sea slugs. Afterword, we can go for margaritas. I know a great spot for both," I said. I made no effort to move. His arms were still on either side of me, and I had no intention of leaving.

"You definitely know all the best spots," he murmured, his lips going to my collarbone. I blushed at the reference to last night. At least I knew he had enjoyed it as much as I had.

"You better believe I do." I leaned my head back, giving him better access to the sensitive skin around my throat as he nibbled down my jaw. At this rate, we would never even make it off the porch. "It's a secret spot, but I think I can trust you."

He gave me one last flutter of a kiss before stepping back and releasing me from the balcony. "I'll get my swim suit."

"I thought I'd interest you in something first," I growled, stepping forward and putting my hands on his chest.

Noah grinned. Snorkeling could wait.

We walked along the sandy path away from the bungalow holding hands. After our morning romp, Noah had microwaved the leftovers from the night before, and we had feasted. I wasn't sure how it was possible, but the pancakes had tasted just as good the next day.

With full stomachs and happy hearts, we headed toward the research station. We walked by the sandcastle we had built the day before.

"Look, it's still up," Noah said, pointing at the castle. Somehow it had survived the tides, and no one had knocked it down. It was still close to being picture-perfect. The idea that the fragile creation the two of us had made was still up and standing made me smile.

We continued down the path, laughing and talking.

Noah pretended to casually bump into me at every opportunity, and I relished it. His every touch was heaven. We walked passed the mangrove peninsula that made up the Grove, cutting through the private property to reach the research facility. It was afternoon now, and I needed to check on the sharks as well as pick up our snorkeling gear.

Noah glanced around as we walked, and I could see him formulating questions for later. I wondered what he saw with his expertise in real estate. The property was considered prime location for the island.

"Any questions?" I asked as we walked.

"I'm on vacation," he answered with a smile. "I'll ask the questions when you're not playing tourist with me. I'll ask when you're back to being the islander."

I laughed. This was going to be a fun day. It wasn't often that I got to play tourist on the island, and I had forgotten how much I loved just visiting places here. I couldn't wait to show Noah my favorite two places in the entire world.

The research station was finally visible as we rounded a corner and cleared the peninsula with the Grove. It was just a small house, but it held so much more than just people. Four research assistants, the Doc, a staggering amount of sea life, and a wealth of knowledge filled the small building to almost bursting.

I looked down at the dock to see the main boat was gone and breathed a sigh of relief. Doc would be out on his dive, and the others had hopefully gone with him. I had the place to myself. It wasn't that I didn't want my coworkers to meet Noah; it was that I didn't want them to give him a hard time. I liked him, and I didn't want them scaring him off.

I turned to see Noah staring at the house, his face blank as if he were remembering something and trying to forget it.

"You okay?" I asked, taking his hand.

He shook himself, smiling as he cleared whatever he was thinking from his mind. "Yeah. Just thinking. Is this where you live?"

"Yeah. I guess you can come pick me up here next time instead of the parking lot," I said. He chuckled. "Me and four others live and work here. If we are able to purchase some land near by, then I'll be able to do my doctorate research program here too."

"What if you don't win?" His voice held a note of concern that made me smile.

"I don't know. I'm trying not to think about it too much. Once we find out, then I'll make a decision as to where to go next. I really love it here, though. I want to stay," I said. I took his hand. "But that is *not* tourist talk. You want a tour? I have to grab my swimsuit."

Noah nodded and followed me in the back door. I couldn't remember the last time I had used the front door.

"Here's the kitchen. There's an attachment over there where we can make the shark food and not get it mixed up with ours," I told him as we entered the house. He nodded, his head on a swivel as he looked at everything. We walked through the "living room" filled with all sorts of fish tanks, and I gave a running commentary on our research and what we did with all of them. His eyes glassed over a little and I hurried him to my room.

I peeked in the door to make sure that Brooke wasn't still sleeping. Her bed was neatly made in the corner, and I gave a little sigh of relief. "Come on in," I invited him. "That's my bed over there."

Noah walked cautiously into the room, going over to my corner. He looked strange standing next to my bed, and yet somehow like he belonged.

"I'm going to change real quick," I told him as I opened the bathroom door. "Make yourself at home."

Noah sat gingerly on the edge of my bed, looking around at my things. I had a poster of the local tropical fish hanging on the wall and pictures of my family pinned below it. He leaned over to look at a family portrait from the last time I was home. A slight smile twitched at the corners of his mouth and I ducked into the bathroom.

I changed as quickly as I could, managing to brush my teeth, put on waterproof mascara, brush my hair, run a razor across my legs, and get in my swimsuit in less than three minutes. I debated between a one-peice swimsuit and a bikini, finally daring to go with the bikini. Even though we would be in the ocean, I was willing to risk losing my suit. I smirked as I thought about the possibility of losing it on purpose with him around. I came out and handed him a bottle of sunscreen.

"If you'll get my back, I'll get yours," I offered, turning around. He quickly stood up from the bed and took the lotion. His big hands rubbed it into my skin in smooth strokes. I had to concentrate on not sighing with pleasure as he did it. "Your turn."

He wiggled out of his shirt, presenting his back to me. Well-defined shoulders merged with the perfect muscles of his back and down into a tight waist. I was sad when I had finished rubbing in the lotion; I could have touched his bare skin for days.

He stretched the shirt over his head as I slathered a little more sunscreen across my face and exposed skin. As he escaped the collar of the shirt, he pointed to the pictures on the wall. "You look like your mom."

"Thanks," I said. I thought my mom was beautiful. "Dad

says Jake and I got her smile, but we got lucky and got his brains."

Noah laughed, the warm sound filling the small room. His blue eyes took me in, checking me out in my swimsuit. For once in my life, I didn't feel self-conscious; I felt sexy. I liked the way his eyes felt on me, and judging from the reaction in his swim shorts, he liked it too. I was all warm and soupy inside because of it.

"Let's go get the gear," he said, taking my hand in his. I had a feeling that a little longer, we would be even later getting to the water.

I guided him back through the house, stopping in the prep kitchen to pick up some fish for the shark pups. Noah eyed the small bucket of fish warily as I led him out to the pen.

"I need to feed the pups before we go out on the water," I said, kicking off my sandals and stepping into the pool. "You want to try?"

"Pups? That's water. Pups are dogs." He stood on the edge looking at the four little sharks swimming lazily around the pen.

I laughed and set the bucket down, stepping out of the pool to take his hand. He frowned, but he slid off his shoes. He followed me until he was knee-deep in the water before he stopped moving. I let go of his hand and kept going. "Just come stand here. I'll bring one to you. They can't hurt you. They're too little."

"Yeah, you say that until Mama Jaws comes to rescue them," he muttered under his breath.

I waded out to where one of the baby nurse sharks was resting in the sun. The little shark let me catch her easily, and I brought her over to show Noah.

I flipped the tiny gray shark over so he could see her tummy. "Look at the spots," I told him. "Aren't they cute?"

Noah raised his eyebrows at the idea of a shark being 'cute', but he looked at her anyway. A little smile came over his face as he saw the tiny, dark polka dots on the creamy underside of the little shark. "They are kind of cute."

"Go ahead and touch them. She won't hurt you," I coaxed. Noah looked at me with his blue eyes big as saucers before reaching out a tentative hand to stroke her skin. The shark held still, letting him caress her.

"She's rough and soft at the same time," he whispered, his smile widening. "What kind of shark is she?"

"She's a nurse shark. Even full grown, she isn't a threat to humans. She likes to eat crustaceans, mollusks, small fish, and stingrays." I turned the shark back over, letting Noah stroke her back. One of the small lemon sharks came over to investigate, but Noah was too involved in the nurse shark to notice. "You want to hold her?"

Noah's smile faltered slightly, but he nodded, holding out his hands. His jaw was tight, but the smile and the excitement in his eyes was enough to tell me he was enjoying the adrenaline rush of holding an apex predator in his hands. I put the little shark on his outstretched fingers.

"How big will she get?" he asked, breathless.

"Up to fourteen feet and seven-hundred and thirty pounds."

"Whoa." Noah stared at the little two foot baby in his hands.

The little shark only stayed for a moment before swishing her powerful tail and swimming off into the deeper water. Noah barked a laugh and pointed at her. His eyes shone with excitement. I loved encounters like this:

letting someone who was afraid of sharks experience them in a safe environment. It was like magic.

"You want to feed them?" I asked.

"By hand?" Noah asked, his eyes widened again slightly.

"Typically. Using your toes just doesn't work as well."

Noah nodded and I went to get the bucket at the edge of the water. "Okay, now hold the fish by the tail and keep that end away from the shark. They do have sharp teeth, and you don't want them to catch you accidentally."

I picked a fish out of the bucket and put it under the water. The little lemon shark that had sneaked over to watch us hold the nurse shark came swimming over to get it, taking it delicately in its jaws before swimming off.

"Was he there the whole time?" Noah asked, a quaver in his voice. He might be a big-shot in other areas of his life, but here he was no longer the top of the food chain. Noah was handling better than many others I had seen.

"Yup." I grinned at him. "He was just curious. Now put your fish in the water. The other one wants his snack."

Noah hesitated for only a fraction of a second before putting his fish in the water. The second little lemon shark swam slowly toward him, waiting until the fish was completely underwater before gently taking the fish and darting away. I didn't know that it was possible for a human to smile that big.

"He was so careful!" Noah exclaimed. "I've had dogs be more aggressive."

"They are really quite smart," I told him, smiling at his Christmas morning level of excitement. "This isn't something you would want to do without me around, though. These two know what's going on. This isn't something everyone gets to do."

Noah looked up and beamed at me. "Thank you. This is one of the coolest things I've ever done."

"You are most welcome." I grinned at him. "Once I feed the nurse sharks, you ready to go out in the ocean and see these guys in the wild?"

Noah swallowed hard, but his grin didn't falter. "If you're with me," he said, his eyes meeting mine, "then yes."

CHAPTER 12

The turquoise waters were calm under bright blue skies as we skimmed along the shoreline in the small boat toward my favorite snorkel spot in the world. To our right, the Grove extended out into the ocean like a finger beckoning a lover. The mangroves turned the water a lighter color as their strong roots dug into the sandy bottom, but they protected the island from the waves of the deep ocean.

Nestled in the shielded curl of the Grove was a small coral reef. It was perfect for much of my marine research, as well as some of the best snorkeling in the entire Caribbean. Only locals knew about this spot, and the pristine conditions of the reef only proved the lack of human interaction. It was untouched by people and absolutely the best place to dive into an underwater world. I couldn't wait to show it to Noah.

I turned off the motor, lowering the anchor onto the sand near the reef and securing the boat so we could swim without worry. Noah stared out at the water's surface, his eyes dancing as he grinned at me. He had his goggles perched on his forehead, causing his hair to spray up like some sort of strange crest. He looked ridiculous, but very excited.

"How is the water so peaceful here? The waves on our way in were fun, but it's like being in a bathtub here." Noah pushed his goggles up further, causing his hair to stand even more on end. It was hard not to giggle.

"The Grove," I explained, pointing to the mangrove trees in the distance. "The mangroves protect this spot from the big ocean waves. It lets the coral grow and is really important during the tropical storms. The reef here usually doesn't get much damage."

"You mean those weedy looking plants?" He frowned slightly at the ugly trees.

I nodded. "Yup. Not only are they the perfect breeding ground and nursery for a bunch of species, they help keep beach erosion down, and they help keep the island safe from storm surges. They are incredibly important to the whole ecosystem of the island."

Noah raised his eyebrows. "Interesting. But they don't exactly scream 'beautiful tourist destination,' do they?"

"No, they are kind of strange-looking." I put my own goggles on my head and managed to keep the snorkel from smacking me in the face in the process. "But I'm glad they don't scream 'tourist'. Tourists tend to think that since they're just here for a short amount of time, nothing they do is going to matter. But there are hundreds of them with that same idea. They take pieces of the reef home as souvenirs; they leave litter and trash; they fish without restraint."

"Tell me how you really feel... don't hold back." Noah held up his hands like he was defending blows from me.

"Sorry." I smiled apologetically. I stopped myself from telling him all about how my fellow researchers and I wanted to purchase the land and turn it into a nature preserve. He didn't need to worry about it, and it wasn't all that interesting. "It's one of my soap box triggers. This is supposed to be fun. This is probably my favorite spot in the whole world."

Noah's blue eyes sparkled like the ocean. He sat on the back of the boat with his feet in the water, getting ready to jump in. "Then I'm honored that you're showing it to me."

"You should be," I teased, pushing him in. He splashed as he hit the water and I followed him into the ocean. It was warm and calm. I took his hand in mine, and together we swam away from the boat and over to the reef.

Coral in the shape of giant fans reflected purple in the sun below us while orange fronds waved smoothly in gentle sway of the water. Colorful fish darted through the rising coral and swaying sea fronds like dancers. Parrotfish with their bright scales moseyed along the reef, watching us with curious eyes. A stingray swam below us in graceful flight before disappearing into the dark of the water. Blue tang, angelfish, trumpet-fish, and myriads of shiny, tiny minnows moved through the reef with amazing ease, filling the ocean floor with color and movement.

Noah pointed excitedly to a hole in a rock where a spotted eel slithered out and went into another section of the reef to find something to eat. Even despite the snorkel in his mouth, he couldn't contain the grin on his face. I dove down to the bottom, picking up a conch shell. It was still very much alive, and Noah held it reverently in his hands. Light pink flesh peeked out of the shell as Noah examined it, and he nearly dropped the living creature. I could hear him laugh under the water as he realized that it wasn't just a shell.

With strong strokes, Noah dove down to the bottom and gently placed the creature on the sand. I smiled at his careful gesture as he made sure the conch was safely settled before returning to the surface. I was glad I had brought him here.

My heart was full of a mixture of sorrow and happiness as I watched him point to a bright blue parrotfish. Noah had said he was only going to be on the island for a couple of days, and I knew he would be leaving any day now. I knew I was falling for him despite my best efforts. Watching him interact with the reef with respect and excitement wasn't helping. It was only making him more attractive to me. I tried to convince myself that just the experience of bringing him here was enough, and that I would be okay not repeating it. Unfortunately, I knew I would want to show him all my favorite places again and again.

Noah came to the surface and pulled his mask from his face, grinning from ear to ear. Together we floated on the water, our hands and feet moving in constant rhythm to keep us steady above the water. His hair gleamed in the sunlight, and his eyes were alive with excitement and enjoyment.

"It's so beautiful down there!" he exclaimed, wiping water from his eyes.

"I thought you would like it," I said with a grin, pulling my own mask up onto my forehead. "Did you see the eel?"

"Yes!" Noah frowned slightly. "You are not getting me to touch it, though."

I laughed. "Good, because I don't think he wants to be touched."

"Unlike some other eels..." Noah gave me a naughty wink. I couldn't stop the blush as I laughed at his dirty joke. He swam closer, his powerful arms easily cutting through the water until he was close enough that we could kiss. "Thank you for showing me this today."

"My pleasure," I said softly as he pulled me into a kiss. The tang of saltwater filled my mouth, his body warm against the cool of the ocean. A heat began to fill my core, surprising me with just how ready I was to have him again.

"I have something I need to tell you," Noah said, pulling away from me. He licked his lips, his blue eyes darkening like deep water. His brows came together, serious and strong. I swallowed hard. He was going to tell me what he did for a living because he was leaving.

"What?" I asked. My heart clenched, not wanting this encounter to be over. I wished I could just stop breathing for a moment and let the ocean swallow me up before he said he had to go. I was far more attached to him than I had planned on becoming. Being attached sucked.

"I'm staying longer on the island."

Hope blossomed, letting my heart beat again. "Really?"

"Yes, really." He smiled, knowing that he had panicked me for a moment. His eyes lightened, and I felt the sun shine again. "It does mean that my assistant is coming out to join me, though. I do have to get some work done."

"Okay," I replied, happiness lifting my voice. He was staying. "For how long?"

"Indefinitely. My job is pretty mobile," he answered with a nonchalant shrug, behaving as if moving to a remote Caribbean island was something people did all the time. "Owen has given me run of the villa for as long as I want."

I squeaked with joy and he laughed. I kissed him and then frowned slightly. "You have an assistant?"

"Yes." He smiled again. "And I wanted to tell you about her beforehand. She's rather attractive."

I raised my eyebrows. "And you're telling me this because..."

"Because I didn't want you to get the wrong idea when

you see her. We aren't a couple," he explained.

"Okay..." I wasn't quite sure what was going on. I was glad he was telling me, but at the same time, the idea of a sexy assistant was rather intimidating. Someone who knew him and would be with him all the time. The boss leaving with the secretary was a popular trope for a reason. "So you have no interest in your attractive assistant?"

"No. And really, I should be more worried about her stealing you away. Not her stealing me away from you." He bobbed gently in the water as I digested his words.

At first, I was more excited about the fact that he had just said I was his. Then the implication of his sentence hit me. His assistant would be interested in me.

"Ohhhh," I said as I realized. Noah laughed.

"She's honestly the best assistant I've ever had, so no stealing her away. I won't have it," he said, trying to keep his face serious but failing. I kissed him on the cheek.

"I'll do my best," I promised. He kissed me again, filling my heart with light. I was his and he was mine. Noah was staying.

"Can I buy you dinner tonight?" He asked once we were back on the boat. I looked up at the sky, seeing that the sun was much lower than I expected. "I'm afraid it won't be much. I have to catch up on some work, but ..."

I looked back at him as he ran a hand through his hair, sending a spray through the air.

"I like having you around," he said simply, a smile on his lips. "You make me happy."

A giddy rush went through me. "You make me pretty happy too."

"So, dinner?" He held his hands open in question.

"I can't," I said reluctantly, shaking my head. "It's my job to cook tonight. You can come if you want. But know that you will be put through the ringer. The boys should be getting back from the mainland and they're itching for all the dirt."

Noah gave me a thoughtful look. "Do you want me to come?"

"I would like you to meet them, but tonight's probably not going to be the best night," I answered honestly. I was surprised that I really did want the boys to meet him. I wanted them to know how wonderful he was and I knew they would approve. However, tonight would be full of discussions about their trip and dissertations, which would leave Noah out of the conversation.

"I'll just catch up on some work, then." He kissed my forehead. "I don't have to worry about them stealing you away, do I?"

I snorted at the idea. They were like my brothers. "Never."

"Good. I would hate having to beat up respected scientists." Noah cupped my cheek and brought his mouth down to mine in a perfect kiss. I loved the way his lips felt against mine, the warmth of his tongue and the gentle caress of his mouth. I kissed him back, pressing my body against his as the boat rocked us gently.

I finally pulled away and started the boat. He sat and watched me with a smile on his face as I steered the boat to the dock at Owen's mansion. The engine and the wind made it difficult to talk, but I was content with my thoughts.

If he was staying, then it meant he cared about me. I could feel the ropes I had tied around my heart to keep it from falling in love starting to loosen. If he was staying, then it wouldn't hurt to let myself have a little more of him. I could easily fall in love with Noah...as long as he wasn't going to leave.

CHAPTER 13

I shut the screen door to the kitchen, leaning on the frame and closing my eyes. I couldn't have imagined a better day if I'd tried. Noah was amazing. My entire being felt light as air and filled with sunshine.

"Have fun?"

I opened my eyes to see Devon standing at the kitchen counter smirking. He was half way through making a peanut butter and jelly sandwich. I had completely missed him when I walked in; my mind had been elsewhere with Noah.

"You're home!" I yelled with a grin, running over to give him a hug. He had taken it upon himself to be my older brother, and I missed him like family when he was away. Devon set down his knife full of peanut butter and wrapped his arms around me. He smelled like sunscreen.

"Hey, kid," he said with a laugh. He was tall and lean with a swimmer's body. The man loved to swim and usually did several miles out in the open ocean every morning. The only downside to his love of being out in the water was that he was of pure Irish descent: pale skin, freckles, red hair, and green eyes. Since moving to the Caribbean, he usually went through a bottle of sunscreen a week and still managed to burn.

"I'm making dinner tonight. Don't ruin your appetite, okay?" I asked, giving his sandwich a pointed look. "I'm making fish tacos."

"Fish tacos! Can Mimi have some too?" he asked, putting the finishing touches on his sandwich. I wasn't worried about him ruining his dinner. The man was always hungry, and if he did somehow manage not to eat his body weight in food tonight, Mimi, his fiancée, would whip something up for him.

"You know I love her. I'd make tacos just to have her come over. You eat your sandwich, I'll hang out with her," I teased. Devon took a big bite of his sandwich and chuckled.

"Lucas is gonna love you for making those tonight." He swallowed and took another bite. "He ate some tacos at a food cart in Miami and then would not shut up for the rest of the trip about how much better yours were. I think he would marry you for those."

I made a face at the thought of marrying Lucas. He too had taken on the role of older brother and protector. I loved him, but I would probably end up killing him on our wedding night out of exasperation.

"Now you're just flattering me," I said, bumping him with my hip so I could get to the sink. "Did you guys have a good trip? How'd the dissertations go?"

Devon leaned against the counter and finished the last of his sandwich. It was a good thing he swam as much as he did, because he ate like a starving man. "Great, actually. Doc had us super prepared. I'm still a bundle of nerves, though." He held out his hands toward me, making them shake.

"Yeah right, Mr. Confidence," I said, sticking my tongue out at him and starting the water to wash my hands.

"Did I hear my little Izzy come in?" Lucas's voice entered the kitchen before he did. He was slightly shorter than Devon, but just as muscular. His particular vice was running rather than swimming. His face was strong and angular with warm brown eyes and unruly dark hair that matched his personality. Lucas was a troublemaker, and he had a knack for practical jokes and being the life of a party.

"Maybe," I replied, pulling ingredients from the fridge.

"Onions, mangoes, peppers, avocados, a bag of marinating fish..." Lucas narrated as I set things on the counter, his voice overflowing with excitement as each one was set down. "You're making fish tacos!"

"Ouch." I glared at him, my ears ringing from his enthusiastic yelling. "I would like to be able to hear tomorrow morning. And yes, I'm making fish tacos."

He wrapped me up in a big bear hug, rubbing his knuckles across the top of my head when he finished. Yup. If I had to marry that man, I would probably shoot him walking down the aisle.

"Let me go," I said after squeezing him back. "Now I have to wash my hands again!"

"Did you hear our little Izzy was out on a date?" Devon asked Lucas, his voice far too innocent. I rolled my eyes. This is why I stopped bringing my dates home.

"A date?" Lucas grinned and batted his eyelashes at me. "When do we get to meet him? Is he coming for dinner?"

"No and no," I told him, pulling out the chopping board. "Hand me the cooking oil so I can start the fish."

"Come on, Izzy," Devon said pulling out the frying pan without being asked. "We're just looking out for you."

"I know." I turned and looked at the two of them. The

three of us couldn't have looked more physically different, but I loved them both as if they were my own flesh and blood. "And I appreciate the two of you being SO concerned, but as much as I *love* having you both involved in my love life... no."

Devon laughed and elbowed Lucas in the ribs. "She thinks we're trouble," he whispered loud enough for the next island to hear.

"On a different topic," I changed the subject, glaring at both of them, "have you guys heard anything about the Grove? I haven't seen Doc yet today."

Both of them shook their heads.

"Nothing so far. There's some sort of new snafu he's having to navigate," Lucas said with a shrug. "Doc's going to be glad you're making tacos. It might actually cheer him up after dealing with lawyers all day."

I frowned and tested the oil before putting the fish in. The fish sputtered in the oil, giving the room the delicious scent of cooking herbs and spices. Both boys' mouths were visibly watering. It was a good thing I had a lot of fish to cook.

"Do I smell someone making tacos?" Brooke asked, joining the three of us in the small kitchen. With two people, the kitchen was cozy. With three, it was slightly crowded. With four, it was claustrophobic.

"Yup. A batch big enough for eighteen," I answered. Brooke stood between Lucas and Devon, playing with a tendril of hair from her ponytail. I did a double-take. She was wearing makeup. Not much, but just a little mascara and eye shadow. I wondered when she had put that on, especially since she had probably been out on a boat all day.

I went to get the big kitchen knife, but Devon was standing directly in front of the butcher's block. I cleared my throat and he blushed slightly, and shuffled to the side. Unfortunately, since everyone had decided to cram into the kitchen, he bumped into Brooke, knocking her off balance.

Brooke stumbled and would have fallen, but Lucas caught her, his hands wrapping around her shoulders to keep her upright. She giggled, and he didn't release her right away. Instead, Lucas got a stupid-happy smile on his face while Brooke fluttered her eyelashes and apologized.

I looked over at Devon and raised my eyebrows, asking him a silent *"What's going on here?"* He rolled his eyes and shook his head, telling me he didn't have a clue, but saw it too. Something was going on between Lucas and Brooke.

I put the onion on the chopping board and then turned to face the three non-helping adults in the kitchen. It was far too crowded for four people, especially when two were so busy flirting they wouldn't have noticed if their shirts caught fire. "All right. Either you help me chop, or you get out of the kitchen." I held up the knife in my hand.

"I think I hear the sharks whining," Devon said quickly, heading to the back door. "I'd better go feed them."

"Right. Be sure to tell them to clean their rooms while you're at it," I said sarcastically. I knew he was really off to see his soon-to-be wife. "Tell Mimi dinner will be ready in thirty minutes."

"Will do," he called back, slamming the screen door behind him. I turned to face the remaining non-helpers.

"I gotta go finish... uh... unpacking. Yeah, unpacking," Lucas stammered, backing away slowly and eyeing my knife. I stuck my tongue out at him as he ducked into the living room.

Brooke went to the sink and washed her hands before going to the chopping board to peel the onion I had set there. I let her have that knife as I pulled out another and started on dissecting the mango.

"So, what's up with you and Lucas?" I asked innocently.

Brooke fumbled with the onion, nearly dropping it on the floor. She recovered it at the last second and set it down. She then flipped her hair over her shoulder like nothing had happened. "What do you mean?"

"Oh, come on, Brooke," I said. I set my knife down and put my hands together under my chin and did an imitation of her high-pitched giggle. "Help me, Lucas, I fell!"

"I do not sound like that!" She squeaked with indignation and smacked me gently on the shoulder with the back of her hand. I gave her a pointed look and she rolled her eyes and shrugged.

"Yes, you do," I teased gently. "Talk to me."

"Honestly, I don't know," she said with a sigh. "You know I haven't had any luck with guys lately. He's been helping me with my hammerhead stuff, and... Iz, I missed him while he was gone."

"And..." I coaxed, finishing my first mango and putting it in a big glass bowl.

"I don't know... you know me and guys. They so much as smile at me and I'm in love." Brooke sliced the onion in half and stared at the two pieces for a moment. "Do you think he likes me?"

"Uh-oh, Brooke," I answered, dropping my voice as low as I could and trying to sound like Lucas. "You fell down. Let me hold you in my big strong arms for ten seconds longer than necessary!"

Brooke giggled. "Fine. Enough about me. What about *your* date?"

"Heaven. With a touch of Perfect." The fish was coming

along nicely, and I started dicing up a second mango, a satisfied grin creeping onto my face.

"Oh, you totally did him!" Brooke exclaimed, jumping up and down a little in a happy dance. Her eyes widened, and she set down her knife so she could put both hands on my shoulders. She searched my face, hazel eyes taking in every detail of my expression. "You have totally fallen for him, haven't you?"

"No!" I told her, shrugging her hands off my shoulders. She raised her eyebrows at me and blinked. "I mean... maybe?"

"Izzy!" she raised her hands like she was going to shake or strangle me, finally deciding on just shaking my shoulders. "I told you, just have fun! He's a tourist! He's gonna leave and I'm going to have to deal with mopey Izzy again. I don't like mopey Izzy. She's no fun."

"But he's not leaving," I justified. There was a thrill in my stomach at saying the words out loud. "He's not leaving."

Confusion twisted Brooke's pretty features. "What? But he's a tourist."

"He's staying longer on the island." I couldn't keep the grin off my face. "He's extending his trip."

"Iz," she said softly. Her shoulders sagged slightly. Her mouth slanted, and I could see her brain trying to come up with a gentle way to bring me back to reality. "It's still just a trip. He's going to have to leave eventually. I mean, that's awesome that he's staying for you, but..." She shrugged.

"I like him, Brooke," I answered quietly. I knew she was only trying to keep me from getting hurt. "I really tried not to. I really, really did. But he's different."

"If I had a dollar for every guy who was 'different,'" Brooke said, grabbing an avocado to slice, "Well, I'd have that Prada bag I want."

"I'm serious, Brooke. He makes me happy." I shrugged and flipped the fish in the frying pan. The room smelled delicious. Brooke silently finished her avocado and put it in a bowl. She set her knife down and wiped her hands on a kitchen towel.

"If he makes you happy, then that's what matters," she said finally, wrapping her arms around my shoulders giving me a good hug. "You know I'll be here for you if you need me. I'll buy the ice cream when he has to leave. Just don't tell the whole island your going with him this time."

A wry chuckle found its way out of my mouth. "Don't worry. I learned that one the hard way." I turned to face her. "Thanks, Brooke."

"For what?" she asked, washing her hands in the sink again. She had a smear of avocado on her cheek.

"For telling me I'm an idiot in the nicest way possible," I explained, "and being my friend."

Her hazel eyes misted for a moment as she smiled. "Well, if I don't tell you you're being an idiot, those meanie-head boys will. Only they'll be..." She thought for a second and shrugged. "They'll be meanie-heads about it."

"Meanie-heads?" I asked. She rolled her eyes and stuck her tongue out at me.

"Shut up."

I laughed and checked the fish. The first batch was done. I set the next batch to go and mixed the mango salsa ingredients Brooke and I had been chopping. All I had to do now was finish the fish and get the tortillas ready.

I turned to see Lucas standing in the doorway. "Um... Brooke?"

Brooke startled and dropped the red pepper in her hands. It landed on the floor, but she scooped it up and quickly went to the sink to rinse it off. I giggled at the two of them trying so hard to pretend to be normal.

"Hi, Lucas. You here to chop some peppers?" I asked, knowing full well that he was there to see Brooke.

"No," he answered, shaking his head. He looked directly at Brooke, his dark eyes nervous. "I was actually going to go check on the shark pups. You want to help?"

I tried really hard not to snort at the blatant excuse. "Hey, girl, come out and look at the beautiful ocean and moon with me!" was really what he should have said.

"Yeah," Brooke answered quickly, nodding and grinning. "I mean, Izzy, do you still need me?"

Brooke begged me with her eyes and bit her lip. I rolled my eyes at her.

"Sorry, Brooke. I'm helpless in the kitchen without you." I stuck my tongue out at her and shooed her with my hands. "Go. I am actually pretty good at making this by myself."

Brooke's face split into a grin about a mile wide as she mouthed the words "Thank you!" I shook my head at the two of them as they hurried through the kitchen and out the back door. Their excitement was contagious. I couldn't help but smile at the thought of the two of them flirting in the dark. It was just too cute. They went well together.

I picked up the newly washed pepper and began to dice it. It was going to go in the salsa. Outside I could hear Lucas's deep baritones punctuated by Brooke's soprano giggling. It was a happy sound. I wondered if I sounded that happy with Noah.

Actually, I thought to myself, *I think I sound even happier.*

CHAPTER 14

$\mathcal{I}$ woke up with the dawn, for once welcoming the warm sunshine instead of hiding beneath my covers and trying for five more minutes of sleep. It was a new day; one that I got to spend with Noah. I climbed out of bed and threw on a bikini that would make Brooke proud and a cute little orange print sundress. Without waking Brooke, who was snoring peacefully with her hair tangled around her head like a halo, I snuck out into the morning sunshine.

I walked along the beach path toward the mansion, humming slightly. I hadn't felt this happy in a long time. I didn't know it was possible to feel this happy. Not only was I off to see the man of my dreams, but he was still on the island. We had a chance.

The sky was a beautiful blue with the only clouds being dark gray, but far on the horizon. The world was made of blue, green, and sand. It was almost too gorgeous of a day to be real. I came to the entrance of the Grove and sent some good vibes toward it. Hopefully that would turn out all right too. I had thrown my four thousand dollars of tip/bet money into the fund to buy it. Four thousand dollars wasn't much toward the overall price of the property, but I hoped it was enough to help tip the scales in our balance. I had already done so much work and had so many wonderful ideas to research there.

Passing the last little bit of the Grove, I came to the beach where Noah and I had built the sandcastle. I almost didn't want to look, afraid that the beautiful castle would be washed into the sea, but I did. And it was still there.

I stepped off the path and into the beach, heading to inspect the sand structure. The moat, and the lack of rain the past few days, had saved it. The edges were starting to wear away, and several of the shells I had placed had fallen into the moat, but it was still standing. Despite the worn edges, I still thought it was the most beautiful castle I had ever seen. It stood on the beach like a glorious sentinel, waiting for its occupants to return from the sea. I wished that it could stay standing like this forever. For a moment, I even thought it had a chance.

I replaced one of the shells and deepened a section of the moat before continuing on my way. I gave it one last look as I got back on the path and hurried on my way to see Noah.

I KNOCKED on the door to Noah's villa, my heart speeding up with every knock. I could hear his footsteps as he came to the door, and I smoothed my hair one last time. I loved how just thinking about him made my insides shiver. I couldn't have removed the grin on my face if someone had paid me.

"Izzy," he greeted me warmly, opening the door. Barefoot, he had on a pair of low slung khaki shorts and a blue t-shirt that made his eyes pop. His hair looked tousled and windblown; it was all I could do to keep my hands to myself and not run my fingers through it. He dipped his head and kissed me demurely on the cheek as I stepped inside.

I had expected the little beach cabana to be empty, but instead, it looked like a paper tornado had hit. Sitting sedately in the center of the wreckage was a petite, adorable, redhead. She had her hair cut in a pixie-cut style that made her sexy and cute at the same time. She wore running shorts and a tank-top that accented her fairy-like body. I was really, really glad Noah had warned me about her. If he hadn't, I would have been incredibly jealous. Even as it was, the green-eyed monster in my stomach wasn't terribly happy about the situation.

"Hi!" the girl chirped, hopping to her feet and holding out her hand. "You must be Izzy."

Her handshake was firm and professional. She grinned, her green eyes sparkling. Her smile was infectious.

"Hi," I replied, "and you must be Noah's assistant."

"Yup, I'm Beth. It's nice to finally meet the woman who has made Noah stop answering my phone calls." She turned to give Noah a teasing glare. He laughed and held up his hands.

"You guys look really busy," I said, eyeing the piles of paper scattered across the table, floor, and chairs. Two laptops sat open on the table, and even their keyboards had paper on them. I tried to see what was written on the papers without looking like I was, but Beth was already busy picking them up.

"Yeah, but I'll take this view over my cubicle any day of the week," she said, gesturing to the ocean out the window. Her arms were full of papers, but she had most of the ones near me picked up before I even had a chance to help. "I should convince Noah to go to his friends' parties more often."

I went to hand her the last piece of paper near my feet; it looked like a map of the island, but Beth had it in her pile before I could get a good look. Maybe Noah was looking at a house to flip? There were several hurricane-damaged properties in the area that he could renovate and sell to a wealthy businessman for a nice sum of profit.

"How about you take the rest of the day off, Beth?" Noah asked, his eyes fixed on me. I bit my lip as he looked tellingly at the hem of my skirt. A warmth spread in my stomach and headed south. "Go enjoy the island a little bit."

Beth set her stack of papers on the table. She grinned at him, her hands busy picking up the various files scattered on the chairs and adding them to her stack. "You don't have to tell me twice. I'm out of here as soon as I get this put away."

Noah put his hand on my shoulder, his touch adding to the warmth in my lower section. He put his mouth near my ear. "Let's go outside and let Beth finish in here," he said, his words causing my hair to tickle my neck and sending sexual currents straight down my spine. I nodded and followed him happily outside onto the porch.

He leaned nonchalantly against the wall. I loved the way his shirt hugged his broad shoulders, then tapered into his waist. He looked good, and he knew it.

"What would you like to do today?" I asked as his blue eyes watched my every move with a slight smile. He looked me up and down, obviously liking what he saw and stoking the fire growing in my belly.

I went to the wall beside him, pressing my shoulder blades into the wood. He shrugged. "I didn't have any plans."

He pushed himself off the wall and placed his arms on either side of me, pinning me in place. My breath caught a little bit. He smelled like clean sunshine and soap with just a hint of something masculine that drove my feminine parts into a frenzy. He came in slowly, taking his time as his mouth covered mine. His tongue probed gently at my lips until I let him in. I heard a low moan that I realized was mine. The man could kiss.

"How's that for doing something today?" Noah asked, his voice low and rough. I wanted him so bad.

"Wow. That sounds good," I gasped. I was already halfway to the bedroom in my head when I heard a thud followed by an "Ouch!" from inside. "I think the room is currently occupied, though."

He chuckled and kissed me again. I wondered if I would be able to walk after this, because he was melting all my bones into liquid desire. He pulled back again, giving me enough space to breathe but still keeping me pinned against the wall.

"Where's she staying anyway?" I asked, desperately trying to gather my wits together. He scattered them so effortlessly that it was difficult. "I happen to know there isn't a pull-out sofa in there."

His mouth twitched in a smile and he kissed my forehead. His eyes were glowing with desire and making my thoughts scatter again. I loved that look. "The main house is practically empty. Owen went home after the party, Jack met a girl on the island, and his secretary is leaving this afternoon."

"Jack brought his secretary?" I asked. "I didn't see her at the party."

"That's because she wasn't invited." The note of disdain

in his voice made it evident he didn't think too highly of the secretary. "The party was just for the boys."

"Oh," I said with a nod. Then I processed the first part of his statement. "Jack met a girl?"

"Inquisitive, aren't we?" he teased, nuzzling my hair. He laughed softly, anticipating my next questions. "She's a tourist. He wouldn't shut up about her. I saw him for all of five minutes before he dashed off to see her again."

"Is that so?" I murmured. I loved the way his lips felt as he nibbled down my neck.

"Oh, Noah, Emma's so perfect! She's so pretty and smart and sexy and..." Noah said, raising his voice several octaves to sound like a girl. I giggled. "It was actually kind of cute, but in a sickeningly sweet kind of way."

"What's the secretary think about that?" I tipped my head to give him better access to my neck. "I'm guessing she wasn't here to work."

"She threw a vase at my head this morning when I went in the house," he said. I pushed his shoulders back so I could look at him, feeling a worried expression shaping my face. He smiled at my concern. "She thought I was Jack." He must have seen the concern in my face, so he followed up with, "Don't worry, she missed."

I punched his shoulder lightly, glaring at him through my eyelashes. He chuckled again and kissed the tip of my nose. "Good. I'd have to go beat her up if she had hit you. Poor girl, getting dumped on vacation."

He pulled back, a frown creasing his face. "Don't feel sorry for her. She brought her pick ax to dig for gold on this trip. She didn't actually care about Jack, and everybody but him knew it." He shook his head as if to banish any further thoughts about her before he smiled at me. "At least this Emma chick seems to like him. He says she doesn't know who he is. That she thinks he's just some guy visiting his wealthy friend on the island."

"That sounds familiar..." I said, exaggerating a thoughtful twist in my mouth and tapping my chin with my index finger. "Handsome man meets girl and keeps his job a secret."

"Ha ha," he said, rolling his eyes at me good-naturedly before going back to kissing his way up and down the side of my neck, his hands pulling my hips into him.

"I'm happy for them," I said softly, pressing myself against him. I could feel him harden at my movement. I really wanted Beth to finish up in there. "You still haven't told me what you want to do today."

"There's a great little touristy area to buy stuff from local craftsmen over by the resort," Beth said, coming out the door. Noah and I both turned to look at her, and she blushed a deep red when she saw the position we were in. "Oh, but you weren't actually asking the question..."

She hiked her very full messenger bag higher on her shoulder, and gave a nervous giggle. I glanced over at Noah to see his eyebrows raise at her. Her face somehow became an even darker shade of crimson.

"Pretend I said nothing. Bye!" And with that, she scurried away and back to the main house. Noah groaned, putting his head on my shoulder.

"Well, at least the house is ours again," I said, arching my back to press my hips into him again. His hands tightened on my waist so I couldn't pull away. He lifted his head and looked into my eyes.

"Actually, before we get to that, I have something I want to give you." His eyes searched mine, and his handsome mouth curled into a smile as if he liked what he saw.

"You don't have to do that," I replied. An impish smirk crossed his features, making him devilishly good-looking.

"Do what?" he teased.

"Give me things. I mean, I know you can afford it, but you really don't have to." I was having a hard time concentrating on our conversation. I wanted to be naked with him, not discussing gifts.

"I know I don't have to." He moved one hand to cup my cheek. "I want to. I want to give you everything."

Before I had time to say anything, he kissed me, his mouth sending me to heaven. I was giddy with happiness. It wasn't the gift that made my stomach do joyful flip-flops; it was that he wanted to give me everything.

He stepped back, releasing me from his grasp and the wall. He grinned, excited like a proud child, and grabbed my hand to pull me indoors. I giggled and followed him, floating on air.

The room was clean of all traces of work. The laptop on the desk had even been neatly stored in a bag off to the side of the room. Noah dropped my hand and held his up for me to stay while he ran into the bedroom. I heard a drawer open and close before he came out, grinning like crazy.

He held his hand out to me, a small silver box with a shiny silver bow resting on his palm. It looked fancy. I took it with trembling fingers. *Please don't be expensive jewelry,* I thought. Since I worked on boats and in the ocean, I could never wear anything nice. I wanted to be able to use this gift, not just leave it to collect dust on my nightstand.

I bit my lip and looked up at him. His eyes danced with excitement as I pulled the bow free and opened the lid. I pulled out the necklace inside slowly. It was a shark tooth hung on a strong, simple black, cotton cord.

He took it from my fingers and undid the clasp before

wrapping his arms around me to put it on. The point of the tooth hung right at the dip of my collarbone. I played with the smooth tooth between my fingers. This was something I could wear even at work.

"The tooth is from a lemon shark," he explained, watching my reaction. "The guy selling it to me told me to get the black cord instead of a chain so you could wear it in the water. Something about it not sparkling."

I smiled up at him. "Barracudas and sharks are attracted to sparkly things," I stated, my brain going into Science Mode without me realizing it. "The flashing looks like a distressed fish to them."

"You are such a teacher," he said with a chuckle. "Do you like it?"

"I love it," I answered honestly.

He put his hands on my shoulders, admiring the necklace. "In the South Pacific, it's legend that a tooth from a man-eating shark will bring the owner a prosperous and long life, free of any evil, especially that of the sea." He shrugged like what he was giving me was nothing special, but the thought was beautiful. "It will keep you safe in the water."

"Thank you," I whispered, lifting my eyes to reach his. He beamed at my thanks and I kissed his cheek. I played with the tooth in my fingers, unsure if I wanted to tell him that lemon sharks weren't man-eaters.

"What?" he asked, frowning slightly. I wondered if he could read my mind.

"Lemon sharks..." I took a deep breath. "They don't eat people."

"You said one bit you." His face split into a grin and he bounced on his toes with glee. He had been anticipating this. "So, while technically it's more of a woman-eater, I'm pretty sure it still counts."

I giggled. "Then it really *is* perfect. Thank you."

I stood up on the tips of my toes to kiss him. I had meant it to be sweet and full of thanks, but as soon as my lips touched his, I wanted so much more. I wanted him.

He cupped my face in his hands, drawing back and smiling. There was sunshine and warmth in those blue eyes, and I couldn't look away. With gentle fingers, he brushed a strand of hair from my face, tucking it neatly behind my ear.

"I love you, Izzy."

My world spun in happy circles. I was giddy and light-headed and about to float through the ceiling with joy. "Really?" I asked, my breath catching in my throat.

He caressed my cheek with his finger. "Yes, really. There was supposed to be flowers and candles..." He frowned slightly at himself. "I meant to tell you in a far more romantic way, but-"

"I love you too, Noah," I said, cutting him off. His face shifted into an ecstatic grin. I loved the way his eyes lit up as he looked at me. I raised my lips to his and we shared a breath before kissing again. "This is more than romantic enough for me."

He wrapped his strong arms around me and picked me up, spinning me in a circle. My feet swung out in a wide arc, our laughter and kisses mingling as we spun. I couldn't believe how fast this was all happening, but in my heart I knew it was all true. Loving Noah was simple and easy. It felt right, like he was always supposed to be a part of my life. Like the universe had meant for us to be together and had just waited until the timing was right. I was happier than I had ever been in my entire life when I was with him. This was what life was all about.

CHAPTER 15

Instead of setting me down, he scooped me up in his arms, carrying me to the bedroom like a fair maiden. He held me gently as if I were a delicate flower, his strong shoulders and biceps not even struggling with my weight. His knees bumped against the big bed, but he didn't set me down. He just kissed me more, holding me close to him.

I wiggled for escape, and he reluctantly released his hold on me with one arm so I was kneeling on the bed, our heads at the same height. He nipped at my lower lip, growling with want. The sound sent an electrical current through me. That noise had the unique ability to send me into a shudder just a millimeter below orgasm.

Not taking my eyes off him, I reached for the hem of my dress, lifting it smoothly overhead. Just before the fabric cleared my eyes, he captured my arms in his. I struggled to free myself, but his grasp was too strong. I couldn't see through the blindfold of my dress, my arms stuck in its straps.

All my senses seemed to heighten with the loss of my

sight. His tongue was wet and hot on my skin as he teased my sensitive flesh and then blew cool air on the wetness he left behind. I shivered, more with want than cold. Noah's breathing was ragged with longing; his every jagged breath made my body ache to soothe his.

"You're all mine now," he growled as I struggled slightly to pull the fabric off my eyes. He strengthened his control over my arms by wrapping the dress tighter. There was no way I was going to escape my cloth confinement.

He kissed me, his lips soft at first, as the two of us melted together like butter. One hand trailed down my outstretched arms, down the curve of my neck, down to the stretch of skin exposed out the side of my swim-top, down to my hip where he undid one of the string ties of my bottoms. The fabric sagged away, barely still covering my nether regions as it clung to my other hip. His fingers gently caressed my bare hipbone. I moaned softly, wanting more.

His hand left my hip, and went to the swimsuit tie at the nape of my neck, and gave it a gentle tug. The top fell forward, exposing me to his gaze. I shifted my weight on the bed, waiting as he looked his fill, my arms still tangled up in the air. He took my left breast into his mouth, making me gasp with the surge of pleasure.

My nipple hardened under his warm, teasing tongue. It was like I had guitar strings running through my body and he was using my hardened nipple as a pick to strum them. I arched my back to give him better access, and he bit down lightly. It wasn't enough to cause pain, but just enough to make my core heat like a furnace.

"Lay back," he commanded. Even if I had wanted to resist, his voice left no room for argument. Happy to give him complete control, I surrendered my body willingly.

I fell to the bed, his arms guiding me down as my own

were still tangled above my head. Once I was flat, he grabbed my hips and pulled me toward him so that my ass was just hanging off the edge of the bed.

"No peeking." That commanding, powerful tone again. Without even meaning to, my arms froze. I wouldn't have lifted that dress off my eyes if I heard a marching band go by. But then again, I was so captivated by Noah that I probably wouldn't have heard a marching band at all. I shivered with anticipation as I contemplated the wonderful things he was going to do to my body.

His strong hands started their caress at my shoulders and worked their way down. Down the swell of my breasts, the curve of my waist and out to the flare of my hips. His touch gave me the most delicious goosebumps. With a quick tug, he released the second tie on my swim bottoms and pulled them away.

I bit my lip, feeling his gaze on me. I wished I could see his face, see what he was thinking. A hand went to each of my thighs and pushed them wide as he wedged his broad shoulders between them. One finger traced the line between my legs that must have been right at his eye level. The promise of what those fingers could do made me squirm with anticipation.

"So wet..." he whispered. I could hear the smile in his voice mixed in with sheer desire. My stomach tightened with want.

"Noah-" I started, but the sentence in my mind was cut off by one perfectly placed tongue, reducing me to a whimpering puddle of yearning. He did it again, taking all my powers of speech. I was lost to the pleasure of his flexible tongue.

He sucked. And nibbled. Tasted and tickled. And drove me out of my mind with want and pleasure.

To be honest, it wasn't a long drive.

The muscles deep in my stomach started to clench and vibrate; the ecstasy was almost too much to handle. Colors started to whirl through my vision and I was barely aware that I was squeezing my thighs together with every ounce of strength I possessed. He didn't stop his tongue from flicking and teasing my poor, swollen nub. Time paused for a glorious, golden moment as I capsized into a sea of pleasure.

When I came back to the surface of the world, I lay there gasping for breath. It was quite possibly the most intense orgasm I had ever experienced. Mind-blowing, earth-shattering, and universe-expanding kind of good. Noah pulled back with a chuckle and planted one last kiss on my still very sensitive, quivering pleasure nub.

His shoulders left my thighs as I struggled to compose myself again. I heard the crinkle of plastic and the sound of his clothes hitting the floor. I wanted to peek so badly, to see his naked body. I wanted to see him ready and wanting me, but I didn't dare move the dress. I squirmed slightly. I was torn between liking the surprise of being blindfolded and wanting to see his handsome body. Maybe, if the dress happened to fall off my face...

"No peeking," he reminded me, pinning my arms again. His body pressed against mine. I could feel him, rock-hard and more than ready against my leg. His body was firm and strong. I arched my hips into him, letting him know that I wanted him as much as he obviously wanted me.

He kissed me briefly, giving me just a taste of his tongue, before rising back up and reclaiming his spot between my legs. My breath hitched as I felt him press against my opening. I wanted to feel him inside of me, joining me. I needed him. Now. But he just teased, giving me just a taste of his velvet length without entering. I arched my hips up to capture him, but he just pulled away and remained just on the edge of my opening. I squirmed with sexual frustration as he toyed with my lust.

I hissed and tried again, using my legs to pull him into me. He evaded me just as easily and had the nerve to chuckle. I was ready to burst into flame with the heat in my core. I needed him so badly. He gave me the smallest fraction of an inch, letting me think I was going to have him inside of me, only to have him pull back. I was being driven mad with lust. Having him inside of me was the only thought in my entire brain.

"Please..." I begged, struggling to find the word amid my longing.

"Say my name," he said, voice low and ready as he poised yet again where I wanted him.

"Please, Noah..." I begged again, arching my hips and reaching to find him. At his name he dove deep, making me cry out in pleasure.

My body responded almost immediately, rising up toward another climax as a result of finally getting what I craved. He pumped again, filling me completely. His hand cupped my breast, finger and thumb rolling my nipple into a tight ball of delight.

"Come for me, Izzy." My name on his lips, the sound of lust and need coursing through it, was enough to send me flying yet again.

Every part of me contracted as liquid pleasure surged through every nerve, fiber and vein. Noah groaned, burying his face in my shoulder as my body caressed his. The addition of his manhood inside me was exquisite and made me fly even higher.

Hands still pinned above me, legs wrapped around his thighs, I called out his name as he pistoned in and out.

Sweat coated our bodies, making us slippery and sticky at the same time. Our bodies collided and found each other in the most amazing way.

Noah released his grip on my wrist and pulled the dress from my eyes. I opened them only to be lost in the kaleidoscope of blue that was his eyes. I wanted to dive into the ring of lighter blue and gold just around his pupils. There was so much emotion in them: lust and something soft, something I was almost afraid of, but desperately wanted. Love. Pure, simple, and true. Love and lust spiraled in blue and gold down into the depths of his soul.

His breathing was ragged, and I felt my heart rate speed into overdrive as his pupils dilated and constricted. I nodded, ready for him. I kept my eyes open, wanting to see him. I could feel him swelling, losing himself, but he didn't close his eyes either.

"Izzy," he gasped as sensation finally overtook him. I watched, transfixed as pure ecstasy filled his face. It was incredibly erotic. I kissed his lips, but he was too enraptured to return the kiss. I loved the way his body was surging and shuddering into mine.

My breath was rough and hard, matching Noah's. The muscles in his arms were shaking slightly, but he didn't pull away from me. He smiled down, all the emotions I had seen before still sparkling in his eyes. If anything, the love was shining brighter.

"I love you," he whispered, planting a soft kiss on my forehead.

"I know," I replied. I had seen it in his eyes. Felt it with my entire body. "I love you, too."

He chuckled softly, the sound masculine and sexy as he nuzzled my jaw with his nose. "I know."

I unlatched my legs from his hips, feeling a tension in

my muscles that surprised me. I was going to be sore later, but I let my feet fall to the floor. He raised up slightly, still connected to me as he pulled the dress from my arms and freed me. I whimpered when he left my body, feeling full and empty at the same time.

His hands went to my waist, and he lifted me higher on the bed so that my head rested on a pillow. The sweat on his chest from our exertions gleamed slightly, accenting each pectoral muscle, each ab, and the delicious V that went down his hips.

He frowned slightly in concentration as he messed with the condom, taking it off and throwing it away. It was sweet how unpracticed the motion was. When he had disposed of it, he joined me in bed, pulling me into his arms and then tracing my skin with his fingers.

I took a deep, content breath in, held it for a moment, and then let it out slowly. I was happy. Thoroughly and completely happy.

CHAPTER 16

My cheek stuck to Noah's chest, the combination of sticky skin and close contact making it so I couldn't leave. I didn't want to. Our bodies were tangled together and wrapped in what was once an orderly bed. I could hear his heartbeat, strong and hard, in my ear as we cuddled and relaxed. I was breathless and completely satisfied. The afterglow was almost as good as the sex.

Noah's fingers traced slow, lazy designs on the bare skin of my back. The ocean shushed at us through the open window after what I knew had been a rather loud session. I didn't care if the mainland had heard us. I was with Noah. He loved me. I loved him. Everything was how it was supposed to be.

For a moment, I let myself dream of the future. Noah loved me, and he wasn't a tourist anymore. He was staying. I hoped it was for a good long time. Or, if he had to return to his work, that he could make the island his home base. I couldn't leave because of my research. My life was on the island. Even if- I mentally knocked on wood- we weren't able to purchase the Grove, I still had work to do here.

But the idea of having Noah with me was thrilling. Even if he had to take business trips, I could live with that. I wondered if he could just do all of his work from the island and make Beth take the business trips. That was an acceptable option too.

I smiled and kissed his skin. This was the beginning of something amazing. I could feel it deep in my bones. Today was going to be the first of many perfect days together. Nothing was going to keep us apart.

Noah's phone rang and startled me. The vibration on his nightstand was surprising, not to mention the old school ring he had chosen as a ringtone being very loud. I peeled my cheek from his chest, giving him and then his phone a very pointed and unhappy look. He laughed and kissed my forehead before twisting his torso to hit the 'Silence' button.

I smiled and cuddled up against his chest again. Our bodies pressed together in the most delicious way, skin touching skin at every opportunity. I ran my hand over his chest, feeling his strong muscles. One of his nipples tightened as I came across it. I kissed the other nipple and felt him tense under me. I wanted another round. I wanted to feel him inside of me again. *If I have my way, we may not leave the bed all day*, I thought to myself.

Unfortunately, his phone buzzed again on the nightstand. He had turned off the sound, but not the vibration.

"Whatever it is can't be that important," Noah grumbled, reaching for the phone to turn it off completely. He hit a button and tossed the phone back on the nightstand before grinning at me. "Now, where were we?"

I grinned up impishly at him. I had some lusciously

naughty ideas of what I wanted to do next. Things that would make my mother blush if she knew I had even thought about them, let alone knew how to do them.

And then someone was banging on the front door.

"Noah?" Beth's voice called from the door. "It's Beth. I need to talk to you."

He groaned and sunk into the bed. I pouted; he shrugged.

"Tell a girl she has the day off, and all she wants to do is work," he mumbled. Beth's knocking was incessant. There was no way we were going to be able to ignore her and get back to what we were doing. Noah made an unhappy noise in the back of his throat and sat up, swinging his legs off the bed. He stood, giving me a fantastic view of his naked body, and picked his shorts up off the floor. I sighed as his perfect ass disappeared into the fabric. At least he didn't put on a shirt.

"I'll be right back." He leaned over the bed and kissed me. I reached up, and made sure to show him exactly what he was coming back to. He made a low sound of masculine approval as he broke away and hurried to the front door.

"Beth, I told you," he said, opening the door. "No business today."

I slid out of bed, wrapping the sheet around my body and peeking out the bedroom door. I couldn't see Beth, but I had an excellent view of Noah's backside. I had plans for that backside... I wanted him out of those shorts and back in bed.

"The lawyers called, Noah. It's happening today. Now." Beth sounded calm and professional, but I could see her words' had a worrysome effect on Noah. He stiffened and ran a hand through his hair.

"Now?" he growled, his voice serious. I could only assume Beth nodded as he added, "I'll get dressed then."

He closed the front door and turned to see me watching him. His eyes softened, and his shoulders dropped a little as he walked back to me. Thunder rumbled ominously in the distance. It sounded like there would be storms this afternoon.

"I'm really sorry, Izzy," he said quietly, pushing a lock of sun-bleached hair from my cheek. "I have to take care of this. It's very important."

I sighed and looked longingly at the bed. So much for never leaving it. I turned back to face big blue eyes. He felt terrible about this. It was written all over his face. I touched his cheek. He had to be able to run his business from here if he wanted to stay on the island. I was willing to do just about anything to make that happen. I would have swum an internet cable back to the mainland if it made it possible for him to stay with me.

"I hate saying that," he said with a sigh and another rake of his hand through his hair. I loved that gesture. It made his muscles pop in all the right places, and he didn't even know he was doing it. "I hate saying it, because it's not more important than you."

I smiled. "You going to tell me what you do for a living?"

He frowned, confusion tightening his brows. "I thought I wasn't supposed to tell you until I was leaving?"

"Well, if you aren't leaving, then go do your job so you don't have to tell me." I grinned at him. His face relaxed into a gentle smile. "I'll get to see you tomorrow."

He wrapped his arms around me in a bear hug, giving me a peck on the cheek. "And many days after that," he whispered. A thrill went through me. I could go for many days.

When he let me go, I dropped the sheet, watching his pupils dilate as he took in the view of my body. Just because I was okay with him working didn't mean I wasn't going to show him what he was missing. His eyes followed me hungrily, the bulge in his pants telling me that he was enjoying the show. I bent over to pick up my swimsuit bottoms and wiggled my ass at him. He let out a quiet sound of pure longing.

"I'm just glad you have a job that you can do here," I said, straightening up. His pants seemed like they were about to bust through the zipper. "I'm glad you don't have to leave."

"Me too," he murmured, his face awash with desire. He shook his head to clear his thoughts. "If I had time, I would show you just how glad."

With that he dropped his shorts. I gasped, feeling my body react to the sight of him hard and ready to go. He winked and shook his head in a slow 'no' before walking to his closet and pulling out a suit. I pouted as he also took out a pair of boxers. Reluctantly, I put on my own bottoms as he dressed.

I gathered the rest of my things and then sat on the bed to watch as he got ready. The suit looked expensive and fit him like a glove. I still loved his naked form better, but he looked damn fine in a suit. He held up two ties as if to ask me which one he should wear. One was blue and the other green. I stood and took the blue one, wrapping it around his neck and easily tying a double Windsor knot.

"Where'd you learn to do that?" he asked softly.

"In high school. My crush was in orchestra with me and could never get his right for concerts. It was the perfect excuse to get to touch him." I smoothed the tie down his shirt. I liked having a reason to be near Noah. "It worked. I got a date out of it."

"Lucky guy," he whispered. I grinned up at him.

"You have no idea. I am the best tie-tyer around." I didn't tell him that the guy had gone on to break my heart when he left for college. It didn't matter so much now.

"You're definitely pretty good at it," he whispered, leaning down to kiss me. "I should let you do all of my ties, too. Beth always messes them up."

Our lips met, soft and sweet. This felt good, like it could become normal. I could get very used to tying his ties for him in the morning. I pressed into the kiss until Beth started knocking on the door again.

"I'll call you as soon as I can," he promised, pulling back but not letting me go. "If I get this done early…"

I went up on my toes and kissed his cheek. "Don't worry about it. I'll help Brooke with some shark-tagging today. Maybe I'll even bring you dinner from Adele's when I'm done."

His face lit up at the idea. "You are wonderful. Fantastic. Amazing."

I gave him a gentle push toward the door. "Flatterer."

He turned and grinned. "Is it flattery if it's true?"

"Noah? You ready?" Beth called through the door. I pushed him again.

"Go to work. I'll see you this evening," I told him as I slipped on my sandals and followed him. His hand went to the knob, but he didn't open it. Instead he just turned and kissed me again.

"I love you," he said simply as he straightened up and opened the door.

"Me too." I stepped out, nearly running into a now very businesslike Beth. She had a full dress suit that made her look professional instead of like a pixie. He winked at me before taking a file from Beth's hands. I grinned at him one last time before turning to head up the path back to the beach. This wasn't quite the way I had been expecting the day to turn out, but as I played with my shark tooth necklace, I figured it was still a pretty damn good day.

CHAPTER 17

Thunder boomed. The air was heavy with the promise of rain as Brooke and I brought the boat into the dock and secured it. Lightning flashed out at the horizon, striking the water with a blinding brilliance. I double-checked to make sure the knots were secure on the boat; I didn't want it floating out to sea with the storm.

"Thanks for the help today, Izzy," Brooke said, heaving her gear onto the dock. We'd had an amazingly successful run. "This data is going to be amazing. If the Grove thing doesn't work out for you, I'll take you on my project in a heartbeat."

"You are most welcome, but I have a good feeling about the Grove. That's where my future is," I told her, securing another rope on the boat. Another peal of thunder made the air shudder around us.

"Yeah, you do mesh better with baby sharks than the big scary ones," she teased. I had done more than all right with "the big scary ones" today, but she was right. I enjoyed the nursery of the Grove far more than the wild of the open ocean.

"You go on in. I'll finish tying up and bring in the cooler." I tossed her the empty canvas bag that had held our lunch.

"Sounds good." Brooke nodded, her light blonde hair catching in the wind and whipping around her face. "Thanks, though. You're the best."

"That's what everyone tells me these days," I replied with a laugh. Brooke picked up the rest of her equipment and hurried down the dock toward the house. The storm was coming in fast. I could see the rain creeping toward the island along the ocean in thick gray sheets. I finished lashing down the rest of the boat, grabbed the cooler, and hurried to the backdoor in an effort to beat the rain.

Thunder shook the windows as I fought the wind to open the kitchen door. The storm was picking up and tossing the leaves of the palm trees around like they were in a crazy dance party. The t-shirt and shorts I had changed into to work on the boat flapped wildly around my body as I struggled with the door. With a loud slam, the wind shut the heavy storm-door behind me, and I set the cooler down. The room was dark and gray, since the light was off and it was so cloudy outside. I ran a hand up to smooth my wind-blown hair, moving the cooler with my foot so that it rested against the wall and out of the way.

"Izzy?"

I startled, looking up at the kitchen entrance. Standing in the doorway to the next room was Doc, his arms unchar-acteristically crossed in front of him. I wasn't sure if it was just the gray light of the storm, but he looked older. Tired. Where I was used to smiles and light, dark lines were now etched into the planes of his face. Something was wrong.

"You scared me," I said, putting a hand to my chest. My heart was pounding, and my palms were suddenly sticky with sweat. The grim look on Doc's face frightened me. "Did something happen to Devon or Lucas?"

"Devon and Lucas are fine," Doc answered. His face crumpled a little, but he did his best to hide it. "I need to talk to you."

He turned and walked into the living room, and I followed. Something bad had happened. Something he wasn't looking forward to telling me. A small table lamp was on in the living room, casting strange shadows on the fish tanks and adding to the deepening sense of gloom. The wind howled outside.

As I entered the room, Devon stormed past me. His face was pale against his freckles, and his eyes flashed with anger. If I hadn't known better, I would have thought there might have been tear marks on his cheeks. He hurried through the kitchen, slamming the door behind him as he went out into the storm. My heart rate ticked up higher. Something was definitely very wrong.

Doc sat down on one of the ancient couches, looking weary and worn. The pale yellow light of the lamp wasn't kind to him and only accentuated the length of his nose and the age of his skin. I didn't see Lucas, but Doc had said he was okay. Nothing could have happened to Brooke in the thirty seconds since I had seen her. Worry clutched at the pit of my stomach.

"What's going on?" I asked, peering through the dark kitchen doorway after Devon. He was probably on his way to Mimi's. I hoped he got there before the rain hit.

"You should sit down, Isabel." Doc's voice was low and guarded. No one called me Isabel. Ever. Unless it was something bad. Something very bad.

"Doc?" I sat carefully on a worn, tan-colored easy chair.

At least, I assumed it had been tan at some point in its life. The chair was probably older than I was.

Doc stared at my feet for a second before looking up. There was defeat in his clear green eyes.

"We didn't get the Grove."

I heard the words, but my brain refused to comprehend them. This wasn't possible.

"What do you mean?" I barely squeaked. "We had enough money... the grants and the donations... and..."

"Someone outbid us at the last minute," Doc interrupted gently. He reached out across the small space and put a hand on my knee. The air seemed to be leaking out of the room somehow, leaving me short of breath. "The lawyers say they can't release who won the bid until the sale is final, but some of the comments they let slip don't bode well. It sounds like a hotel company."

The foundations of my world were crumbling. The Grove was supposed to be my project. My future. I had so many hopes and dreams for research, conservation, and education, and they were all fading before my eyes. If a hotel company had bought the land, the Grove was going to be destroyed. There was no way a fancy tourist hotel would want the mangroves taking over their beach front property. It had happened to other mangrove groves in too many places to count. They would raze the Grove to get at the beach underneath. The island's government wouldn't stop it, because another hotel would bring in more tourist money.

"Izzy?" I noticed that Doc's eyes were rimmed with red. This was painful for him too. He had devoted years of his life to studying the ecology of the area, not to mention the thousands of dollars and man-hours he had put forth to try and make the Grove a nature preserve. This was as much a blow to him as it was to me.

"I'm so sorry, Doc," I whispered. Details were suddenly all I could see. Doc was wearing a frayed green shirt that had a small hole in the left sleeve. The couch he was sitting on had a miniscule stain in the corner of the center cushion. The light in the third aquarium was flickering. My mind was trying to focus on anything, on everything, other than the news.

"It's not your fault, Izzy," Doc comforted. He was handling this better than I was. I could barely breathe. The air was now completely gone from the room. Doc peered at me, a frown of concern deepening on his already lined face. "Are you going to be okay?"

"No," I gasped, standing up far too quickly. The room spun. Thunder shook the windows, further disorienting me. I stumbled against the end table with the lamp. The room swayed in the movement of the light. I was going to be sick.

"Izzy, it's going to be okay." Doc's voice was distant, but somehow his hands were on my shoulders. I didn't want his comfort. I wanted to rage and scream and cry. It wasn't fair. This wasn't how things were supposed to be. Everything had been perfect this morning, and now it wasn't.

Noah. He was still perfect. Things were better when I was with him. I knew he couldn't fix this, but I needed him. I needed him to hold me and lie and say that things would work out better in the end.

I shook off Doc's hands, twisting away from him and banging my thigh against the table. It was going to leave a bruise, but the pain felt far away.

"No, no, no..." I chanted, weaving my way out of the living room and into the kitchen. Doc was just a couple of steps behind me.

"Izzy," Doc called, grabbing my arm and spinning me to face him before I ran out into the storm alone. "Where are you going?"

"Noah."

Doc let me go and nodded. "Be safe."

I ran from the kitchen, slamming the door behind me. Wind whipped at my hair and sand bit my skin, but I didn't care. I almost wished it stung more so I could forget the sick sensation in the pit of my stomach. I ran from the house, my feet pounding on the cement as I headed for Noah's place.

There was too much and not enough in my mind. The Grove was going to be destroyed. I was sliding out of control and had no brakes to stop me. Months of planning, fundraising, meetings, and hoping were for nothing. Everything I had worked for, everything Doc had worked for, was going to disappear into a monstrosity of a hotel.

The storm hit the coast with a hiss. Gray sheets of rain cascaded against the sand as it made land. I didn't care. I kept running down the path until I hit the Grove.

I stood in the pouring rain, staring at the tangle of wood and brackish water. It would never be considered classically beautiful. It wasn't what people expected of a tropical island paradise. But it had been my passion. I had seen myself in that Grove.

Logically, I knew I would recover. This wasn't the end of my career, but for this moment, this second in time, it was a knife in my heart. I ran past the Grove, the sobs heaving in my chest. It was all going to go away. The green and brown murky depths would no longer stand guard over the fledgling fish and sharks. The birds would have to find somewhere else to live. It felt so wrong that something so important to the local wildlife could disappear so easily. I would have to find somewhere else to chase my dreams.

The only problem was, I didn't *want* to find somewhere else. I had already become attached to those gangly trees. I had planned my future around them, and now it was changing. I didn't have a good plan for this. I had been too hopeful, too optimistic that we would be successful.

I couldn't see anymore. I stopped to wipe my eyes, unsure if it was rain or tears obscuring my vision. There was only one person who could make me feel better. If I could just get to him, then I could forget about it all for a little bit. Tomorrow, when the sun was out and the sea was calm, I could tackle this. I wouldn't be so raw with emotion and loss. I could handle this tomorrow if I had Noah tonight.

I started running again, the world a smear of gray rain across gray sand and ocean. The green of the Grove had ended. Another pang hit me. Our sandcastle was gone.

I could see it crumbling under the incessant pounding of rain, melting back into the beach. It was no longer beautiful. It was ruined. Destroyed. The fact that it too was going away broke my heart. *Nothing gold can stay...*

I picked up my feet and started to run again, needing to find a release from the pain.

CHAPTER 18

I ran hard all the way to Noah's door. His window was open despite the storm, and I could hear his rich laugh from inside followed by the higher birdsong of Beth's. The rain had eased up slightly, but the world was still painted in shades of gray. Night was coming. With ragged breaths, I pounded my fist on the door and waited.

He opened the door, a smile on his face. His suit jacket was off, and his white dress shirt was open at the throat, the tie undone and resting on his shoulders.

"Shit, Izzy," he exclaimed, concern quickly replacing the smile. "Are you okay? What's happened? What's wrong?"

He stepped out of the doorway and into the rain, his hands going to my shoulders. They were almost hot against my skin after the cool of the rain. Raindrops fell on his white shirt, plastering it to his skin and making the fabric translucent. His eyes were blue oceans of caring, taking me in and letting me lose myself.

"They sold it..." I sobbed, the words coming out in a jumble of syllables and sounds. I wasn't even sure if they even sounded like words. "It's gone... and..."

Noah wrapped his arms around me, pulling me in to him. "Shh," he whispered, stroking my wet hair. "I'm here."

I buried my face in his shoulder. His shirt was now soaking wet, from both the rain and holding a sopping girl in his arms. He didn't seem to care. I sobbed into the fabric of his shirt, finding strength in his embrace. In his arms, I was safe and warm. The storm couldn't touch me here. The world couldn't destroy this.

"I'll be back in the morning," Beth said quietly, slipping past Noah and out into the rain. Her face held only sympathy. Noah gave her a nod as she hurried to the main house. He held me close and squeezed me tightly.

"Come inside," Noah urged gently. He brought his hand to my face and wiped my cheek with his palm. "Let's get you out of the rain."

I nodded meekly, letting him guide me into the house. He closed the door behind me, and I stared at the floor. I was dripping all over. The rain was quieter now, making a soothing sound on the roof. I hugged my arms around me and looked up. There was an open bottle of champagne on the table. Noah and Beth had been celebrating something.

"I'm sorry," I whispered, staring at the bottle. Noah followed my gaze and then put his forefinger under my chin, his eyes soft and kind as he looked at me. "You have work. I can go..."

"No," he said firmly with a shake of his head. "My work is done for the day. It was actually a good work day for me."

I smiled weakly. "At least it was good for one of us."

He wrapped his arms around me again, giving me strength. He was so warm I didn't want to let go of him. Ever.

"If today wasn't good for you, then it wasn't good for me either." He released his hold on me, still keeping physical contact as he turned me toward the bathroom. I was eternally grateful he hadn't asked for more information yet. I wasn't ready to say the words out loud to someone. Maybe if I didn't explain to him that the Grove had been sold, it wouldn't be real. He took my hand in his. "Let's get you dried off."

He took two steps, but I didn't follow. I stared at the tile floor, then at his feet, up his legs, up his chest, up to his eyes. He was so handsome. He was everything I wanted in a man.

"Izzy?" His eyebrows raised, concern evident in his every feature.

"Make me forget," I whispered. "Make me feel better. Just for a little bit."

A tear slid down my cheek. Now that I was out of the rain, it felt hot on my skin. Noah towered over me, protective and strong as he came back to get me. He didn't say a word, just put his hand under my chin and tilted my face up to meet his. His kiss was soft, but there was a burning need behind it. There was heat and spice at the edges. I could lose myself in him, and that was exactly what I wanted.

I opened my mouth, my tongue questing for his. I was insistent. I was pure need.

He responded in kind, nipping at my bottom lip and then soothing the sting with his tongue.

I grabbed his tie in both hands, balling the silky fabric in my fists and pulling him in to me. He kissed me harder, thrusting his tongue into my mouth and tightening his grip on my hips. I hoped there would be bruises. I wanted bruises.

I let go of the tie and started to fumble with the buttons on his shirt, my hands slippery with the rain. Instead, Noah just reached down and ripped his shirt open, sending buttons flying in all directions. I could hear the quiet plastic tings as they scattered across the floor.

I kissed his chest. His skin was damp from the rain, but warm against my lips. His nipples were hard and small, either from the cold or my kisses. I didn't care why. I was letting my body do all the thinking, forcing the cerebral part of my brain to shut up.

Noah's hips pressed into mine, and I could feel him hardening. I let my hand graze the growing bulge in his pants, and my conscious brain stopped thinking. This was what I wanted. This was what I needed. This would take my mind off of the things I couldn't control.

He wrapped his arms around me, and together we stumbled toward the couch, not even making it to the bedroom. We were beings made of nothing but passion and longing. At the last second he picked me up and tossed me onto the couch with a growl. His face was dark and almost frightening with lust as he towered over me. I swallowed hard.

He kicked off his pants, flinging them into a corner of the room. His poor boxers were about to split at the seams. My core heated, and every lady part I owned quivered with desire. I licked my lips, wanting to taste him again.

"Nope," he growled at my gaze. "My rules."

He reached for my shorts and roughly ripped them from my body. A fond smile crossed his lips, his eyes still dark as he took in the brightly-colored bikini bottoms from earlier. One finger caressed the slippery fabric, sending shivers up and down my spine. He hooked his fingers around the edges and pulled them off, not bothering to untie them this time.

I struggled out of my shirt, half hoping he would catch me in it like he did earlier, but he let me escape the cloth confines without incident. His hands went to my breasts, fingers digging into the soft tissue. I groaned, enjoying the feeling of his muscles behind it. He wasn't being gentle, and I was enjoying the sense of escape it was giving me.

I pulled the tie at the nape of my neck and then contorted my arm behind me to pull at the bow holding the back of my suit together. The fabric crumpled into Noah's hands and he threw it across the room with a snarl. He dropped to his knees next to the couch as I lay down.

One of Noah's hands went to my breast and squeezed while he attacked its twin with his mouth. His fingers twisted and squeezed while his teeth bit and lips sucked. The little slivers of pain were a delightful contrast to the pleasure and only made it more intense. I gripped at the back of the couch, arching my naked body into the sky as he pleasured me.

With one last pinch, Noah's hand ran down my stomach and to my inner thigh. He pushed my legs open, settling the pad of his thumb directly on the button to my pleasure center and began making small circles. I dampened instantly. First one finger, then two glided in and out on that wetness as he continued to nibble on my tender nipple. I arched my hips into his hand. He started slow, but was soon using the strength of his arm to slam into me.

I cried out as he bit down again, sending a jolt of electric heat deep into my stomach. His five o'clock shadow was rubbing the pale skin of my breast raw, but I loved it. It gave me one more sensation to lose myself to.

His hand was moving hard and fast, whipping me toward climax. I wanted rough. I wanted him to use my body and make me forget my problems. His hand was certainly making me forget. I was climbing toward an intense orgasm. I was going to come, and I was going to come hard.

My body started to shake as the first wave hit me and Noah somehow increased the intensity of his fingers. The sensation of falling, of spiraling out of control overtook me and I lost my thoughts to sensation. Pleasure consumed me.

Oblivion didn't last as long as I wanted it to, and I was back to panting for more. I needed to forget. I needed Noah inside of me to do that.

I sat up on the couch, grinning wickedly at the surprised look on Noah's face at my quick recovery. With a smooth motion, I left the couch and straddled his hips, pushing back on his shoulders so he that he'd lay down. He resisted slightly but then let me have my way. His erection was already trying to enter me, even with his boxers still in the way.

I opened the fly of his boxers, letting his rock-hard cock emerge. He seemed to try to stop me, but he didn't have much of a choice. Before he had a chance to protest, I began to slide my body down onto him. As he penetrated me, my hands went to my hair, and I moaned as I threw my head back. When I looked down, I saw his eyes seem to roll back in his head as he let out a low, masculine groan. I liked it. I liked having this kind of power over such an alpha man. It was powerful and heady to know I could have that affect on him.

I began rocking my hips, undulating like a snake. His nipples tightened further, and his hands went to my hips. I took one of them in my hands and brought it to my lips, putting his thumb in my mouth and sucking. His eyes opened, and he stared up at me with heated, dark eyes. Those blue eyes were coals of burning desire. I grazed my teeth across the pad of his thumb before placing his hand squarely on my breast. He grinned and began to knead it with his fingers.

I started to bounce up and down, slamming his length deeper and deeper inside of me. The hand not on my breast when to my front, finding my swollen nub. He pinched it, rolling it between his fingers and then flicking it. I wasn't ready for that kind of sensation and my whole body suddenly seized. Instead of climbing the mountain of pleasure slowly like I usually did, I was helicoptered to the top and pushed off the edge. My whole body rocked and spasmed, every nerve on fire with pure ecstasy.

I collapsed in a boneless slump against his chest, gasping for breath and shaking.

"You're not done yet," he growled, pushing me up and sliding out from under me.

I rose to my hands and knees, still dizzy with pleasure. He positioned himself behind me, his hands firmly on my hips. I screamed his name as he pushed into me. The new position felt deeper. He could pound into me with more strength, and I willingly welcomed him.

His hand went to my hair, balling it into his fist and pulling back hard. I arched my back and cried out. He was in complete control. I struggled slightly, fighting against the dull ache in my scalp, but he just tightened his grip.

Smack!

A delicious tingle of pain shattered my world as his hand came down on my bare ass. The pain was like the bitter in chocolate to bring out the sweet. He brought his hand down again with another ear-splitting smack that made me arch my back further and cry out. I hoped there would be a red hand print later to bear testimony to the wonders he was working on my body.

The skin tingled as he gently traced his fingers across the offending area. My nerves were made of fire now. Even the gentle caress of his fingers was heightened almost to pain. I loved it and craved more. I could barely remember my own name, let alone what had happened.

Behind me, Noah's hand tightened in my hair as his rhythm increased. My body was responding to his. It was primal and full of need. I was going to crest again. I had never experienced anything like this before, but I wasn't about to complain. I wasn't sure if it was the spankings, the hair-pulling, or the sheer primal need radiating off of Noah in waves that was doing me in, but I loved it.

Together, we rose and shattered, his groans and my cries mingling into a song of shared desire and release. We were lost to everything but each other. Nothing else mattered but the way Noah's body filled mine. The way his breath came ragged and hard, his legs taut and thighs pressed into mine. The way his fingers dug into my hip and pulled at my hair. That was all that was mattered.

After a moment, he sagged against my back, releasing his iron grip on my hair. I gasped for breath and dropped to my elbows.

"Sorry," he gasped, as he pulled back. His voice was strained and rough.

"For what?" I asked, rolling onto my back to look up at him. My mind was a delicious haze, and looking at him only made it better.

"No condom." He ran his fingers through his hair and frowned. I sat up and kissed the smooth skin of his sternum.

"I'm on the pill. Besides, I didn't give you much of a choice," I said, smiling. His face relaxed into a self-satisfied grin and I lay back onto the floor. "That was amazing."

"Who said I was done?"

My stomach tightened with heat and need. I looked up at his smirking mouth and raised eyebrows.

"What else do you have in mind?" I asked. I was already heating at the possibilities.

"I intend to make you forget everything but my name,"

he whispered, a wicked smile curled on his face. His eyes were dark coals again, and my body trembled in excited response.

Who needed to remember anything but his name? I thought. I certainly didn't.

CHAPTER 19

$\mathcal{N}$oah's dark hair caught the edge of the morning sun and gleamed. I stared at it, watching as the light slowly illuminated his sleeping face like he was an angel. He was snoring gently, and his face was soft and peaceful. I couldn't get over how handsome he was. Or that I was in his bed. I had a gorgeous, charming, and amazing man who wanted to give me gifts and would hold me and let me cry. Not only was he attractive, but he was kind and sweet too. I was the luckiest girl in the world.

Except for the fact that the Grove was going to be destroyed. I sighed and relaxed my head back into the pillow. I kept watching Noah's serene sleep. He had been so generous and kind the night before. It was only because of him that I had slept. The ache in my heart at the loss of the Grove was still fresh, but at least the immediacy of the shock had worn off. In the light of day, I could deal with it. I still had a future. I still had Noah. Things would work out. I was stronger than this little setback.

My stomach rumbled, reminding me that I hadn't eaten anything since lunch the day before. Careful not to wake

Noah, I slipped out of bed. I found one of his t-shirts in a drawer and put it on. It smelled like his soap. I was wrapped in Noah, and it made me smile. Before heading to the kitchen, I tucked the curtain closed so that he could continue sleeping.

The fridge was unfortunately empty. A bottle of mustard, two pickles, and something I hoped wasn't a lab experiment in penicillin were all I could find. I closed the door and opened it again, hoping the contents had changed. They hadn't.

A thought struck me, and I grinned. Adele's was open. I could go get breakfast from her, and bring it back for Noah. It would be a nice surprise and a great way to say thank you for taking care of me. It was perfect. I could already see his smile as I gave him her cinnamon roll French toast with a side of banana crepes.

With quiet steps, I sneaked back into the bedroom and grabbed my clothes. Reluctantly, I took off his shirt and carefully folded it back into the drawer. I would put it on again when I returned, but it was way too big for me to wear out. Noah sighed contentedly in his sleep and turned onto his side. I beamed good dream thoughts his way for a moment and then hurried out to go get breakfast.

Outside, the birds were singing in the sunshine. The world smelled of fresh rain and clean soil. The storm had washed the world. Everything was bright and new. Like my future. There were other possibilities I could explore now. At least, that was what I told myself as I walked.

I came to the turn in the path to get to the restaurant and made the mistake of looking at the beach where our sandcastle had been. I couldn't stop my feet from heading toward the water. The castle was gone. Destroyed. All that remained was a mound of white sand. Even the shells had been scattered by the rain, wind, and waves. My chest ached with the loss.

I bent down to touch the sand, feeling the fine grit between my fingertips. Maybe today Noah and I could come back and rebuild it. Make an even better one. I smiled at the thought. It was just what I needed. To rebuild something and make it even better. If I could do it with a sandcastle, then I could do it with my research. I could start again.

I dusted off my hands and stood, feeling hopeful for the first time in hours. With a smart turn, I ran headlong into the reporter whom Noah had been trying to avoid. I stumbled back, apologizing and feeling suddenly off kilter.

The woman was beautiful up close. She was thin, but with curves in all the right places. Her khaki shorts showed off firm, strong legs, and her bright blue v-neck shirt gave just enough hint at cleavage to draw the eye. She wore sensible, but pretty, sandals today instead of spiky heels. Dark hair spilled attractively around her shoulders in soft waves. I could see how she had gotten exclusive interviews with powerful men. It was hard not to look at her and be impressed.

She smiled, but there was no warmth in her eyes. They were shark eyes. Predatory. And I was now the fish she had set her sights on.

"No hiding from me this time," she said. Even her voice was sexy. "You care to make a statement, Isabel?"

"How do you know my name?" I asked, thrown completely off balance. I smoothed my shirt self-consciously. It was an old shirt that smelled like sunscreen. Normally, that didn't bother me since that was the best thing to wear out on the boat, but standing next to this perfect, model-like woman, I felt incredibly inadequate.

"It's a small island. I asked around." She shrugged and

tossed a lock of silky hair behind her shoulder. "Contrary to your boyfriend's opinion, Danica Lewis is actually pretty good at her job."

So she was one of those types of people who referred to herself in the third person. Awesome. She definitely had confidence in spades.

"No comment." Isn't that what all the people in the movies said? I didn't want to talk to her, so I side-stepped her and returned to the path.

"No comment?" She made an incredulous noise. "The man you're sleeping with goes and buys your nature preserve out from under you, and you have no comment?"

I froze in my tracks. "What?"

The woman sashayed over so she could face me. She raised perfectly groomed eyebrows in mock innocence. "Oh, you didn't know?"

"What are you saying?" I asked. The world was threatening to spin out of control again. I couldn't handle another life-changing shock this soon. I wanted her to be lying. I wanted to walk away and not hear what she had to say, but my feet didn't move.

"Noah Black, owner of Diamond Hotels, just bought the property that you and your scientist friends wanted to turn into a nature preserve." She smiled smugly.

"I'm afraid you have my Noah confused with someone else," I said, forcing my feet to take a step forward. She blocked my way.

"There's no confusing Noah Black with anyone but Noah Black." She smiled with her perfect lips. She had a bone, and she wasn't going to lose it. "You do know he's going to build timeshares on the property, right? I can't imagine you'd be too happy to see the flux of people coming in and out of those. I hear that's hard on the local ecology."

I didn't want to talk to her. I didn't want it to be true. I hadn't eaten yet, and I wasn't ready to deal with another giant problem until I at least had a cup of coffee. I started walking, bumping her with my shoulder when she didn't move out of my way. It couldn't be true.

"He didn't tell you who he was, did he?" She called out. I tried my best to ignore her, but her voice cut through me like butter. "He's charming, isn't he? Makes you laugh. Feel comfortable. You trust him instinctively. Enough that you didn't even feel the need to figure out what he did for a living."

I stopped. I didn't want to believe her words, but the little voice in my head was listening. She hadn't said a single thing that wasn't true yet. *But she hasn't said anything that she couldn't have guessed*, I argued with myself. She walked slowly to my side again.

"Did he tell you about the trial?" she asked, her tone seductive. "Or did he say he didn't want to talk about it because he liked the way you looked at him?"

Her words hit their target. I swallowed hard. That was almost exactly what he had said.

"Don't feel bad. He's done it before. The land-stealing part. That's actually what the trial was about." She shrugged as if it meant nothing. I stayed quiet, and she took it as her cue to continue. "It was a couple of years ago, but the parallels to this are interesting. Basically, he found out, through a lovely girl like yourself, that some prime real estate was up for auction. The girl wanted to turn it into a bird refuge and was getting donations to do so."

My heart was pounding so hard I could barely hear Danica. She had to be mistaken or lying, and yet her story rang true.

"Anyway, he bought it out from under her. There were

some issues with zoning, but the man's made of money and just bought everyone off." She moved so she could look at me better. Her lipstick was perfect and made her mouth lovely to watch, much the way a cobra is beautiful before it strikes. "Sounds familiar, doesn't it?"

She waited for me to say something, but I remained silent. This couldn't be true. It couldn't.

"There was some question as to the legality of what he had done. The girl sued him, and their case went to trial." She brushed a windblown strand of dark hair off her cheek. "I was there for the whole thing. I'm actually surprised you didn't recognize him. It was all over the news for weeks. Such a scandal."

I faintly remembered seeing something about a hotel land-buying scandal on the news, but I hadn't paid any attention to it. It was one of those news stories that was always on at the oil-change place. I had watched it more because there was nothing else to do for thirty minutes besides read old magazines about cars. Could that really have been my Noah? Could the man who had comforted me, let me cry on his shoulder, and held me like a child been the one to do this? There was a small voice in the back of my mind, the one that always thought the worst of everything, that whispered yes.

"He didn't win the lawsuit, by the way." Her eyes watched my expression like a hawk. I knew my face was betraying my every thought, but I tried my best to mask them. Her lips turned up in a sinister smile. "He settled. Which means, he knew he was guilty. He knew. Just like he knew he was buying your property."

I cringed like she had punched me in the gut. Anger started to swell. I didn't have to listen to her lies. She just wanted a news story. A nice quote to go above her byline. I knew my Noah. I knew he wouldn't have intentionally hurt me. It had to be a different Noah. It had to be.

"I don't have to talk to you," I said crossly, forcing my feet to move forward. She stepped back and held out a business card.

"You're right, you don't. But here's my card in case you change your mind," she said, voice smooth as honey. She moved out of my path, and I didn't take her card. "But, I know more about Noah Black than anyone else. He's not what he appears to be. I thought you should know."

"Thank you for your concern," I replied, sarcasm dripping from every word as I walked faster. If I got to Adele's, I would be safe. I could think there without her bothering me. Adele would make sure I was okay.

I hurried into the restaurant and took a deep breath, inhaling the soothing scent of baking sugar and butter. It was still early, but Adele's was starting to get busy. Danica had followed me up the path, but she wasn't coming in the restaurant. I had a moment to think.

"Hey, honey," Adele greeted me, setting a carafe of coffee on an empty table and coming over to give me a tight squeeze. "I heard about the sale."

I sighed. The news was out. "Did you hear who bought it? Doc didn't have much information last night."

Adele's sweet face smiled gently, her eyes full of pity. She patted my cheek before turning and picking up the morning paper from a recently vacated table. I had to read the headline twice.

Diamond Hotels Buys Island Property. Next to the article was a picture of Noah, smiling and dressed in a trendy business suit with Beth in the background. My heart sank. It *was* my Noah.

I scanned the article, feeling tears form behind my eyes. The lump in my throat threatened to suffocate me.

> *Noah Black, President and owner of Diamond Hotels has purchased beach front property on Key Island. An inside source confirms that hotel/condo plans have already been drawn up and submitted.*
>
> *This comes as a blow to local scientists who had been hoping to turn the property into a nature preserve and conservation area. A city council member, who has asked to remain nameless, stated that, "the increase in tourism and tourism related dollars is worth far more than another nature preserve. We are simply looking out for the economic well being of our island."*

I handed the paper back to Adele, my hands shaking. I didn't want to read any more. I actually couldn't because of the tears I was struggling to keep inside. Adele held the paper up and frowned at it.

"Isn't this the man you came in with the other day?" she asked. My stomach clenched.

"Yeah. It was." I felt like my life was on repeat. Yet another tourist was breaking my heart and making a fool of me in front of the community. Only this time it was way worse.

"And he didn't tell you he was buying the land?" Adele pressed.

"No, it didn't come up," I said sharply and instantly felt bad. This wasn't Adele's fault. I didn't need to take this out on her. I needed to go home. I needed to think. "You know what, Adele? I'm actually not hungry. I'm just gonna go home."

Adele nodded and wrapped her arms around me again. She smelled like cinnamon. "I understand, dear."

No, you don't, I wanted to tell her, but I just smiled meekly and quickly broke away. I couldn't get out of the restaurant fast enough.

The door closed behind me and I gave serious thought to going back in. Waiting patiently for me in front of the restaurant was Danica. I wanted to punch the smug smile off her face. She had seen me look at the paper through the window, and I could only imagine what was going through her head.

"Leave me alone." I glared at her and turned to walk in a different direction, but she just moved to intercept me.

"Why do you think he stayed on the island after the party?"

"I told you to leave me alone." I clenched my jaw and worked my fingers into a ball. I really wanted to hit something, and she was looking like a good target.

"Did he tell you it was because of you?" she asked sweetly. "Because, if I were you, I'd think it was so he could sign the papers before you and your scientist friends had a chance to do anything."

The truth struck me like a baseball bat, but I didn't want to give the evil reporter the satisfaction of seeing me break. I couldn't breathe again. The air was too thick to get past the lump in my throat and the knot in my chest. I was glad I hadn't eaten anything, because if I had, I would have been sick right there.

"I'm not going to give you a sound byte," I said, doing my best to keep my voice level. I even impressed myself by managing to keep it steady. "Leave me alone."

I pushed past her; every muscle in my body was wound

too tight. She moved out of my way, eyes dark and full of derision.

"If you think he'd do the same thing for you, you don't know Noah Black," she called after me. I ignored her, focusing on putting one foot in front of the other. I needed to get to where I could think and cry. I needed to be alone.

The buying of the land, I almost could have forgiven. I hadn't said anything about it to him, and I could give him the benefit of the doubt. But it was the rest of what Danica had said that irritated me and rubbed like salt in a fresh wound. It had truth to it. Why else would he stay on the island? Bring his personal assistant? He needed to be on the island for the sale. I was just a convenient way to pass the time. That thought hurt more than the loss of the land. I wasn't sure if his love for me was real or just a comfortable lie.

I hurried up the walk to the house, desperately trying to keep my tears at bay. One of the boats was missing, and I hoped that meant everyone was off on an expedition. I wanted the house to myself. I just wanted to curl up in bed and pretend this was all a terrible dream. I was going to wake up and find out that Doc had gotten the property and that Noah was here for me and not his business. Things were going to be the way they were supposed to be, which wasn't like this. This had to just be a bad dream.

CHAPTER 20

The house was mercifully quiet as I stumbled to my room. I opened the bedroom door and felt a rush of gratitude that Brooke's bed was empty. I had the place to myself. The sob I had been holding in finally escaped as I clicked the door shut and slid down to the floor. I felt so heavy with betrayal I couldn't stand anymore. Everything hurt. How could he have done this to me? He had said he loved me! I had loved him, and truthfully, I was still in love with him.

Every beat of my heart hurt. I cried into my hands, sobs wracking my body with every strangled breath. I wished I could stop breathing and just let the heartache die out. I wanted to cry until I was empty and it didn't hurt anymore, but somehow I just kept finding more tears.

I cried until my butt went numb from sitting on the floor, but even then, I still felt miserable. There was a box of tissues on my nightstand. The bed looked like a better option than the floor. At least there I could cry myself to sleep. With far more effort than I had expected, I hauled myself away from the door and up onto my bed. I felt a little better with a cleared nose and a cushioned bottom, but not by much. *Small steps*, I told myself. *Small steps.*

"Izzy? You okay?" Brooke asked, carefully opening the door and peeking in. She must have heard me crying. She saw me and my new pile of tissues and gave me a sympathetic look. "We'll figure something out with the Grove and your research. It'll be all right."

"I never should have fallen for him, Brooke. I should have listened to you." I looked up at her, fresh tears welling up in my eyes. I could tell her to go away, but knowing Brooke, that would only make her nosier. It was better just to get it out now. At least then she'd go buy me ice cream.

"What?" Brooke closed the door behind her and knelt on the floor by my bed. "What'd he do?"

My chin quivered. "My Noah is the Noah Black who bought the Grove. He used me."

Brooke's face went pale. Then red. Then pale again. Her mouth opened, and she worked it silently for a moment as she decided which emotion she wanted to feel first. She finally settled for shock as she stood up and wrapped her arms around me. We could be angry together later. That's why I loved Brooke. She was always there for me.

"Oh, Izzy," she whispered in my ear as she hugged me close. Her hand ran down my hair to my back in a soothing, petting motion. "I'm so sorry."

The words were still bitter in my mouth. My Noah was Noah Black... A heaviness descended on my soul. I had said it out loud and made it a reality. Until that moment I had hoped that it wasn't, that if I didn't say anything, by some sort of strange magic, it wouldn't be true. But it was. My Noah was the one who had bought the Grove. My Noah was the one who was going to destroy my research and dreams. And my Noah wasn't here because he loved me.

With Brooke's comforting arms around me and my world teetering on crumbling apart again, I started to cry. Brooke didn't say anything. She just held me close and rocked me gently, like a child. I cuddled into her, wishing I was still small enough that I could hide under my blankets and make the monsters disappear.

CHAPTER 21

"*Izzy* doesn't want to see you." Brooke's voice drifted through the open window and interrupted my nightmares. I was in the Grove running from a giant backhoe that was ripping it up. Noah sat in the driver's seat and laughed as he chased me. I was glad to wake up and find I was safe in my bed and not running and tripping on mangrove roots.

I sat up in the dim gray of twilight with a blanket tucked neatly around me. My face was crusty with tears, and my ribs ached from sobbing. My laptop was still open on Noah's Wikipedia page but set neatly on the desk. I must have fallen asleep crying, and Brooke had tucked me in and saved my computer from falling off the bed. I stood up and tiptoed through the living room to stand at the entrance of the kitchen.

Devon and Lucas were sitting stiffly on the couch pretending to read. They were doing a lousy job at it, though. Their ears were practically falling off their heads with how much they were straining to listen. I couldn't blame them. Devon flexed his fist a couple of times. At least

I knew if I wanted Noah beat up, they would happily hold him down so I could hit him.

"Please, I just want to see her. She just left this morning and won't pick up her phone. I just want to make sure she's okay." It was Noah's voice. Just hearing it made my whole body hurt.

"Okay?" Brooke sneered. "You sold her out. She had her heart wrapped up in the Grove, and you stole it from her to make it into something she'll hate!"

"I didn't know!" he shouted back.

Brooke made an exasperated noise. "Right, sure you didn't. You need to leave."

"Please," he begged. "I just need to talk to her. Just for a minute."

I went to the screen door and looked out at him. Brooke was standing on the edge of the porch, not letting him step foot on it. She reminded me of a rather fierce poodle I had been terrified of as a kid. Noah's eyes met mine through the screen door, and I took pity on him. His hair was a mess, as if he had repeatedly run his hands through it and it had gotten stuck, and his eyes had a lost look to them. He was right. I had just left. I hadn't given him the opportunity to explain himself. I owed him at least that much.

"It's okay, Brooke," I said, opening the door and stepping onto the porch. My voice sounded ragged and rough. I looked right at him. "You get one minute."

Brooke crossed her arms and shot him a glare that should have killed him where he stood. She stalked across the deck and grabbed the screen door from me. "I'll be right inside if you need me."

"Thanks," I whispered. Brooke put her hand on my shoulder and gave me a long look. *Be strong,* she said with her eyes. I nodded. I had been played a fool for the last time.

The door shut with a click. I knew Brooke, Devon, and Lucas were listening intently inside. They had my back.

"What do you want?" I asked, crossing my arms.

"Izzy, I swear I didn't mean to buy it out from under you," Noah answered quickly. He put one foot on the porch and I glared at it until he put it back on the ground.

"I realized this afternoon that I never actually said anything about it to you," I said. I hoped my voice sounded as cold as I wanted it to. His expression brightened slightly, but I hardened my eyes. "But I did tell you how much the island needs that grove. How bad tourism would be for that reef. That I remember very clearly. Are you going to build condos over the Grove?"

"The tourism will be good for the island," he answered. His hopeful expression was fading quickly.

"Right." I tightened my arms. "I made my stance on that pretty clear as well. You can leave now."

I turned to walk back into the house. This conversation was over. He didn't care about me or the Grove. The next thing I knew, though, he was on the porch, his hand around my wrist to keep me from going inside. My traitorous body responded longingly to his touch. I still wanted him, wanted his hands on me.

"Please let me go," I whispered, frozen in place by heartache.

"Izzy, I love you. I want to make this right." There was a note of desperation in his voice. His breath caught and looked at me with sad eyes. I pulled my arm out from his grasp.

"Then don't build the condos. You still have time to reverse the sale." I held my breath as I waited for his response. He didn't answer. He just frowned and looked at my feet. I knew then that we were very much over. We probably should never have been together in the first place. "But, obviously, the money is more important to you. More important than I am. I get it. Your ex-fiancée would be very proud of you."

His eyes shot up, flashing with a blue fire. I didn't care. I knew I was hitting below the belt, but I didn't care. He deserved it.

"Oh, yes, I did a little research on you." I thought of what I had found on his Wikipedia page and what he had said on our walk. I knew this was a sore subject. I knew this haunted him. And I was very willing to use it. "After your fiancée left you for someone with more money, you started making all sorts of shady deals. It worked because you're a billionaire now."

Noah's breathing sped up, and two spots of color grew in his cheeks. My breath hitched in my throat for a second. It wasn't like me to be mean, to say things out of pure spite. But at that moment, I didn't care. He had hurt me. Obliterated my dreams. A girl's entitled to a little bitchiness when she's heartbroken.

I laid out my last blow. "I'm sure she'd be happy to be with you now. Internet says she's single. All she cared about was money and now you've got it. You two deserve each other."

And with that I turned on my heel and opened the door to go back inside.

"Izzy..." He said my name like a plea. I looked back at him. His blue eyes were shining with tears and hurt. He held his hands out in front of him like he was asking for forgiveness. I had none to give.

"I don't think this is going to work out, Noah." That was the understatement of the year. "You need to leave. Please don't try and see me again."

I stepped inside the safety of the house and closed the door. I couldn't believe I had actually said those things out loud. I had wanted to hurt him like he had hurt me. Brooke took me into a hug as soon as I cleared the kitchen.

"Izzy! Please!" Noah called out, banging on the door. At least he had enough sense not to open it. Devon and Lucas were on their feet and at the door in a heartbeat with murderous expressions on their faces.

"She asked you to leave," Devon growled through the door. Lucas crossed his arms and glared daggers behind him. Together they looked scary as hell and completely blocked the door.

"Izzy..." Noah's voice cracked. I turned my head away from him and into Brooke's shoulder. She tightened her arms protectively around me.

"We're not going to ask you again," Lucas stated. He sounded deeper and bigger than usual. And definitely not happy. The porch creaked as Noah took a step away from the door.

"I didn't mean to hurt her. I do love her," he pleaded with the boys. I was glad I couldn't see his face.

Devon snorted. "You've got a funny way of showing it. The Grove was her life. And you're going to tear it down to make money you don't even need. You're a billionaire. An extra couple million isn't going to do anything for you. You don't need the Grove like she does, but you're more than willing to put your bank account ahead of her. So, I'm gonna go ahead and say that you don't really love her. That's not what love is."

"Yeah," chimed in Lucas.

I could have kissed Devon. And even Lucas for standing up for me. They loved me, in their own unique ways, and I loved them right back. They really were my older brothers.

I could hear Noah reply, but his words were lost to me. I didn't care what he said anyway. Devon was right. A new hotel on the island would only make him richer, and if his Wikipedia page was correct, he wasn't exactly hurting in the money department. The funds he had spent purchasing the land, and even the figures he would eventually make on the investment, was barely a drop in the bucket for him. The island was too remote to ever be more than a luxury destination. This hotel was all about prestige.

And he wanted that prestige more than he wanted me.

"You okay?" Brooke asked. I realized I was shaking.

"Yeah." I wiped at my eyes and smiled weakly as Devon and Lucas entered the room. "Thank you, guys."

Devon scooped me up in a big bear hug, squeezing me to within an inch of my life. "You deserve better," he whispered as he let me go.

"Hey, you want to get a drink?" Lucas offered, raising his eyebrows. "My treat?"

I smiled at him. Lucas had to be seriously worried about me if he was willing to buy. It was sweet. "Thank you, but no. I just want to go lie down for a little bit."

"Okay, then." Brooke nodded and put her hand on my shoulder. She gave it a gentle squeeze. "If you need anything, you know where to find us."

I nodded and put on my best fake smile. It was pathetic and they all knew it, but they let me go. As I opened the door to my room, I looked back to see Lucas take Brooke's hand in his. I hoped they'd have better luck than I did. At least they knew what the other person did for a living.

The room was mercifully dark. I crawled under the sheet and closed my eyes, waiting for the sweet relief of sleep to come take me.

CHAPTER 22

I kicked at the covers until I freed my feet from their tortuous grip. My bed was a disaster area; I had tossed and turned all night with nightmares. Dreams of the destruction of the Grove. Dreams of Noah. Dreams of what could have been. The early morning sun was starting to peek through the blinds, and I was relieved to see morning and be free of my subconscious mind's twisted wanderings.

Brooke mumbled something into her pillow. She was spread eagle across her bed and still fast asleep. I gave serious thought to just staying in bed all day and moping, but the longer I lay in bed, the more I needed to get up and stop thinking. And at this point in time, thinking was bad. Thinking reminded me that not only had I lost the Grove, I had lost Noah as well. Just thinking his name made my chest tighten and the tears start to well up in my eyes. I still couldn't believe he was willing to give me up that easily.

I sat on the edge of my bed and ran my fingers through my hair, trying to figure out what to do next. The shark tooth necklace lay neatly on my nightstand. I had considered throwing it away, but I couldn't bring myself to part with it. Instead, it rested in a perfect circle on my nightstand. I swallowed down a lump in my throat the size of a cruise liner, quickly looking away and pulling harder at my hair.

I needed something that would keep me busy. Tagging sharks with Brooke? I looked over at her snoring into her pillow and knew she wouldn't be up for at least a couple more hours. Besides, she was still inputting the data from our last outing. Who else? Lucas and Devon would be busy working on their grants, and Doc would be helping them. I knew they would do something with me if I asked, but I didn't want to be a bother. I was on my own today.

With a sigh, I stood up and grabbed my brush. My hair was just too tangled to un-knot it with my fingers. I frowned at nothing in particular as I worked the brush. I wanted to go outside. Sunshine always made me feel better. With that idea planted firmly in my head, I put on my one-piece swimsuit, a pair of board shorts, and a light t-shirt. I grabbed my swim bag with snorkel gear, sunscreen, towels, and various other items and went to the kitchen.

Brooke had made me deviled eggs, bless her wonderful soul. I popped one in my mouth and tried to send her a telepathic 'thank you.' She knew the way to mend my broken heart: food. I carried the plastic container holding the rest of the eggs with me out the door so I could continue to snack on them. I didn't have a clear plan as to what I was going to do next; I just knew I needed to get out of the house.

The smaller boat bobbed gently at the end of the dock, drawing my attention. The boys would be busy with their grant work today, so I could take the boat out. I could stay close to shore, but no one would bother me out on the ocean. I could be free. Saltwater and wind sounded like the perfect salve for my soul. My feet were down the dock before my brain even registered that was what I was deciding to do.

I sent a text to Brooke and Doc that I was taking the boat, then turned the ignition key. It felt good to be out on the water. The sun glittered off the sea, and the boat skidded along the waves, bouncing just enough to make it fun. A pod of dolphins followed me out into the ocean, jumping and dancing alongside me like faithful friends. They lifted my spirits.

I suddenly found myself at the Grove. I hadn't been paying attention to where I was going, and I had just followed the dolphins as they played beside me. I turned off the engine and gave the pod a dirty look. One dolphin jumped up beside me, and I swear he giggled before swimming off back into the ocean. If I didn't know better, I would have said those trickster dolphins had brought me here. This is why I liked sharks.

Speaking of, I could see a large lemon shark pup swimming through the pale green water between the roots of the mangrove trees. He would be big enough soon to swim in the open water, but for now, he was still hunting in the protected shallows. A heron called from deeper inside the dark green trees. I let the boat drift as I watched the edges of the roots. Small, colorful fish flitted in and out of the dark roots while crabs skittered on the dry portions. This was where life grew.

I saw two tiny lemon shark pups waiting under a large root structure. They were far too small to survive out in the open ocean, but here they were safe from predators. I watched them, mesmerized. One caught a small fish and ate it in a single bite. He was a strong little guy. I hoped he survived the destruction that was going to occur. I knew he wouldn't, though. Even if construction was a year away, he would still be too small. A larger shark or fish would eat him up in an instant without the protection of the mangrove roots.

It broke my heart.

I didn't want to look anymore. It was too beautiful here, and knowing that it was all going to go away hurt too much. I glared out at the direction the dolphins had swum off to. Stupid dolphins bringing me here.

I sighed. It wasn't entirely their fault. I drove that route often enough with them riding my wake for it to be habit for all of us. They didn't know that everything was going to change. In their watery world, nothing had changed yet. I envied them.

I needed something else to do. Something productive. Something that would make others happy. I felt the corners of my mouth twitch upward as it came to me. The fish tanks needed cleaning; this was Lucas's job. So did the storage areas by the shark pools; that was Devon's. The kitchen could use a good scrubbing, and the yard would benefit from some attention; these were Brooke's and Doc's respective chores. I turned on the boat and headed home. If I couldn't be useful on my research, then I would be useful to the people who cared about me.

NINE HOURS, four scrub brushes, one broken broom, three garbage bags of leaves, and one and a half bottles of cleaning solution later, the entire research facility was clean. We kept it pretty clean anyway, but now, it practically sparkled. I had cleaned every tank, organized and swept the storage area, dusted, vacuumed, and cleaned everything I could get my hands on.

I sat on the couch, watching the reflection of light in one of the now pristine fish tanks. I was exhausted physically, but somehow my mind hadn't gotten that memo. My hands ached from scrubbing, but I knew if I went and lay down for bed, I would just think of him. His kiss. How his hands felt on my skin...

"The house looks awesome, Izzy." I startled as Brooke broke into my thoughts. She glanced around appreciatively. Lucas was right behind her as they emerged from the kitchen. I could smell something delicious baking in the oven. It was Lucas's night to cook, but I was sure Brooke had helped him out. The man usually made sandwiches for dinner because he could barely make toast without burning it.

"We should have you break up more often," Lucas said. "I like not having to do any chores."

Brooke smacked his chest with the back of her hand and shot him a dirty look. "Hey! Be nice."

"What?" Lucas asked, genuinely confused for a moment. Then he looked at me and laughed nervously. "Sorry, Izzy. You know I didn't mean it like that."

"I know," I replied softly. I knew he was just trying to lighten the mood with a joke. That was just what Lucas did. He flopped onto the couch beside me and put his arm over my shoulder. It felt nice, and I laid my head on his shoulder. He gave me a gentle squeeze.

"Dinner will be ready in forty-five minutes. Doc and Devon should be back by then," Brooke informed me. She raised her eyebrows at us all cozy on the couch. "I'm going to go take a quick shower. Don't make out with him while I'm gone, Izzy. No matter what he says, it will not make you feel better."

"Yes, it will," Lucas countered quickly. "I'm like a broken

heart Band-Aid. Kissing me will make you lose all your troubles."

"Unfortunately, it would also make me lose my lunch," I quipped, making a gagging motion. Brooke laughed and shook her head as she headed toward our room.

"You want me to go beat him up?" Lucas asked quietly once she was gone. I shrugged.

"I don't know. It's super tempting."

He gave me another squeeze. "I know. I'll hold him down and you can hit him. Brooke will totally be our alibi."

"Alibi? I don't want to *kill* him." I frowned at Lucas. He grinned.

"Then we are making progress. Not wanting to kill your ex is a good sign. We'll have you forgetting his name in no time." Lucas grinned wider as I cracked a smile. He gave me a real hug with both arms this time.

I sincerely doubted that I would ever forget Noah, but smiling had felt good. Life was going to go on. Heartbreak couldn't last forever.

"You smell like fish," Lucas informed me, pulling back and making a face. I rolled my eyes at him.

"What do you expect? I did all *your* chores," I said, feeling more lighthearted. Lucas had that affect on people. He was annoying as hell, but he knew how to pick a person up. "I'll shower when Brooke finishes."

"Good, you need it." He pinched his nose and made a face. I just rolled my eyes again.

"I'm going to go feed the sharks. At least they don't care how I smell," I said, rising to my feet.

"Be careful they don't mistake you for a fish," he called out as I headed to the back door. I considered making an inappropriate hand sign in his direction, but I knew he would enjoy that too much.

Outside, the air held the sweet promise of evening. The sky glowed purple as the last streaks of red and orange shifted into dusk. The heat from the day still lingered, but with the sun tucked firmly in bed beyond the horizon, it was just a radiant heat instead of demanding. I loved this evening time. The nocturnal world was just coming alive while the day prepared to rest. It was a magical time where anything could happen.

The waves shushed gently in the distance. With the oncoming night, the sharks were active. I watched them for a moment as they glided through the water. They were regal. Kings of the water, even as pups. I kicked off my sandals and stepped into the cool water.

A tingle of electricity went up my legs. I loved being in the water with the sharks. They were still dangerous despite their size, and I craved the surge of adrenaline I felt by being with them. If anything could make me forget my heartache, it was these guys.

I went until the hem of my shorts brushed the water. The larger lemon pup swam close, and then back to deeper water. My little sharks weren't quite so little anymore. The plan had been to release them back into the Grove this week, but with the impending destruction, I hated the thought. They might be big enough to survive when construction begun, but I had grown attached to them. I wanted them to make it and not just possibly survive. They deserved the best chance they could get and I wasn't sure it was at the Grove anymore.

I skimmed the surface of the water with my fingers, watching the moonlight catch and shimmer on the ripples. There was another mangrove outcropping further down the island. It didn't have as large a reef, or as good a placement on the island, but it was an alternative for their release.

Unfortunately, it wouldn't work for my thesis. I swallowed down the anger rising in my throat. It just wasn't fair. The Grove was just so perfect for my research and the island.

"You love them, don't you?" Noah asked, his voice soft in the darkness. I startled and turned around quickly to see him on the edge of the pool. He looked handsome in the moonlight, softer and more romantic. It terrified me. The irony that I was in a pool with sharks and I was terrified of leaving it was not lost on me.

"You shouldn't be here," I said. I was proud that my voice didn't waver, even though I was shaking like a leaf. I wished he would go away, but at the same time I wanted him to stay. As much as I wished it wasn't true, I still loved him. One day of heartbreak wouldn't take that away.

"I couldn't sleep last night," he replied, ignoring my statement. His eyes were dark pools as he watched me. "I just kept dreaming of you."

He took a step closer to the water and slid out of his shoes. I stared at his bare feet, hoping that he would come closer and praying that he wouldn't. I stayed silent.

"So, since I couldn't sleep, I went for a walk last night, and I found myself at our sandcastle." His hands were behind his back. He wore a dark blue polo that accentuated the strength in his shoulders and displayed his beautiful arms. "The rain had pretty much washed it all out to sea, but I could still see it. I realized that it was the most beautiful thing I had ever built."

When he stepped into the water, my heart threatened to burst out of my chest.

"I have hundreds of spectacular hotels. Architectural jewels and historical treasures that I've turned into five star hotels, but that sandcastle was the most beautiful thing I have ever built because I made it with you," he explained.

He took another step. I held my breath, waiting to hear what he said next, wishing my own heartbeat wasn't so annoyingly loud. He pulled his hands out from behind his back and presented me with a small, glass bottle. "This is my message in a bottle. I've been stranded on an island of money, and I didn't even realize it."

I took the bottle in my shaking hands. It was the shape of a small bottle of wine and made of clear glass with a cork stopper. There was sand and a rolled up piece of paper resting inside of it.

"Will you read it?" he asked quietly. His voice held hope and desperation. I looked up from the delicate glass to see his face. Moonlight shone in his eyes, fear and concern sparkling in their depths.

I pulled the stopper out, and carefully picked out the piece of paper with my fingers before replacing the stopper. I unrolled the paper, being cautious not to drop it or the bottle in the water. Despite my care, I nearly did when I read it. It was the deed to the Grove.

"It's yours," he said, answering the question in my eyes. "It should have always been yours. I should have made the connection, but I was too wrapped up in securing another amazing business deal to realize what I was doing to you."

I opened my mouth, then shut it. I didn't know what to say. I needed to sit down, but I was in the middle of a pool and he was blocking my exit. I carefully rolled the paper up and put it back in the bottle. My breathing was ragged, and my heart rate was out of control.

"I need to ask you something," I said quietly, desperately trying to sort out the tangle of emotions in my chest.

He took a step closer so that we were almost touching. I looked up into his eyes and saw nothing but honesty. "Anything," he whispered.

"Why did you decide to stay on the island?" The question had been burning into my very being ever since Danica had mentioned it. I needed to know.

"For you," he said simply.

"Not to buy this?" I asked, holding up the bottle containing the deed. He shook his head and smiled softly.

"I could've bought that property just as easily from my office in New York. I stayed for you." He paused and slowly raised his hand to my cheek. "I'll stay for you."

My breath caught in my throat. Raw emotion washed over me in waves: shock, happiness, relief, hope, and finally love. I couldn't stop the tears from running down my face as I smiled up at him, seeing the same mix of emotions reflected in his blue eyes. I didn't know if I kissed him first, or he kissed me, but somehow our lips met and the world righted itself.

I kept my arms wrapped around him when we broke apart for air. I never wanted to be separated from him ever again. Noah's eyes were bright with tears of joy as he kissed my forehead.

"Why is there sand in here?" I asked, shaking the bottle gently. The grains of sand made a peaceful sound against the glass. The sharks swam near our feet.

"It's from our castle. The foundation was all that was left," he explained. He locked eyes with me. "That's where I'd like to start with you again."

I smiled, losing myself to the warmth and love in his eyes. I nodded, not trusting my voice. Instead I kissed him, pulling him into me with love and desire. I let my kiss tell him that was what I wanted too. His kiss told me he understood.

EPILOGUE

I take a deep breath and let it out as slowly as I can. All that does is make me feel lightheaded as the butterflies in my stomach continue to dance around. I smooth my wedding dress one last time and try to be patient. I feel like I've waited forever for this day, even though it's only been barely a year.

"You ready?" Brooke asks, poking her head inside the door of the bridal villa. Her hair is done up in an elaborate bun. "It's show time!"

I nod and she grins, closing the door behind her. I try the breathing thing one more time, but I'm still nervous. My dad takes my hands in his before I can smooth the satin of my dress again.

"You look beautiful," he says. Memories fill his eyes as he looks at me like he did when I was a little girl playing dress-up. "I'm so proud of you, Izzy."

He hugs me, careful not to mess up my hair. It crunches slightly from all the hairspray, but the curls remain intact. Dad puts his hands on my shoulders and looks me up and down. His eyes are brimming with tears, but he's smiling.

"Thanks, Daddy," I whisper. I'm glad he's here. My entire family arrived a week early to enjoy the island and meet my soon-to-be husband. I think they love him as much as I do. Mom and my little brother are out waiting with the rest of the bridal party. I can't believe how big Jake has gotten since I saw him last. He's practically all grown up.

"You ready?" he asks, tucking my arm into his. I'm not sure if he's the one shaking, or if I am. Probably both of us.

"Definitely." I grin. I've been waiting for this day for a long time.

The sunshine is bright as we step out of the villa and onto the sandy path leading to the beach. I can hear the string quartet playing over the gentle murmur of the waves. The wedding planner holds up her hand as we get to the aisle. Dad squeezes my arm.

The music changes. My heart is pounding. It's time. The wedding planner grins and motions us forward. My father guides me into the aisle, and we begin to walk.

There are smiling faces on either side of me: friends, family, relatives, and all the island locals. Devon and Mimi grin as I walk by them. Mimi is about ready to pop from her pregnancy, but she is radiant. I remember how beautiful she was at their wedding, and I hope I look the same. Lucas flashes me a big thumbs up. He proposed to Brooke two weeks ago. Doc is sitting with Adele and Dominic. Adele is already openly crying.

But there is only one face I want to see. Noah's.

He is standing at the altar, waiting for me. He looks so incredibly handsome in his light gray suit against the white of the sand and blue of the water. His hair, for once, looks tamed and combed. I wonder how many times he's tried to run his hands through it today. Our eyes connect and I can see all the nervousness leave his shoulders. He smiles, and I'm captured in his gaze. His eyes are so blue, they call to me like sirens. I stop walking and start floating. This is it.

"Who gives this woman to be with this man?" the minister asks.

"Her mother and I," my father replies. His voice shakes a little. I know he's practiced that line all day. My mom wipes her eyes and beams up at me from her seat.

I hug my father. His lips brush my cheek, his eyes glistening with happy tears. His little girl is all grown up. He shakes Noah's hand, and then, reluctantly lets me go.

Brooke takes my bouquet and gives me a wink. She's grinning like a fool. Noah's hands are strong and steady on mine. He smiles and we turn to face the minister. I'm glad I have Noah's hand. With him there, I don't shake so badly. He is my rock. Together, we can face anything.

Noah squeezes my hand. "Thank you for coming."

I squeeze back. "I wouldn't have missed this for the world."

We promise to love one another. We promise to support one another. I know that we will do these things. We already have. We have been doing it for over a year now. There are no secrets anymore. Only honesty and love. Our foundation is strong; we are ready to build our sandcastle.

The ceremony is a blur. All I know is that I am happy to promise my life to Noah. His blue eyes shine with joy as he promises the same to me.

"You may now kiss the bride," the minister tells us. I can't believe we're at this part already. I grin and Noah cups his hand on my cheek. The smile spreading across his face tells me everything I need to know: we are going to be happy.

The crowd cheers. I can hear my little brother whooping and Lucas's distinctive, annoying wolf whistle he enjoys using. They are happy for us.

We part from our kiss, breathless and grinning. The crowd is still cheering. Noah takes my hand and raises it up in victory. We have made it. The crowd roars even louder. My brother starts imitating Lucas's whistle technique. Together we hurry down the aisle.

We escape to a quiet spot just off the path, and Noah pulls me in for another kiss. This one is ours. We take our time, enjoying our moment away from prying eyes and cheers. There will be many more kisses tonight, but this one is special.

"I love you," Noah whispers, his forehead pressed against mine.

"I love you," I tell him and he grins. "You ready for the fun part?"

"I thought we were saving the private villa with champagne and strawberries for later, but if you want to skip the reception and go do that, I don't mind," he teases. I give him a gentle push, and he laughs.

We take the necessary photographs--the ones that I will treasure for years--while the rest of the guests head to the yacht for the reception. Noah let me see it yesterday, and it is a floating ballroom and restaurant. I am excited to celebrate. My face hurts from smiling, but I can't stop. This day is perfect.

Onboard the yacht, the party is getting started. The DJ announces the wedding party, and then for the first time, Mr. and Mrs. Noah and Isabel Black. I like the way that sounds.

We enter the room to the sound of applause. I look at everyone who has come to celebrate with us. We take our time and walk around to the various tables. My mother hugs Noah as my father congratulates us. Lucas and Jake grin mischievously from across the table. I wonder if it was a good idea for the two of them to meet.

Jack and his fiancée Emma congratulate us. Logan, Robbie, and Evan all shake Noah's hand and make him laugh. Jack asks if he can get a Naughty Shirley Temple later.

When he sees I haven't noticed it yet, Noah points me toward the center of the room where the food is. I gasp. The centerpiece is a giant sandcastle. It is an almost perfect replica of the one we built so long ago. It's beautiful. I step closer and realize that there is more to it than just the towers and seashells, though. The moat is shallow and filled with some sort of glass to make it look like water. Swimming through the glass are sharks made of sand. Lemon sharks.

I laugh in delight, and Noah's face splits into a wide grin.

"You like it? I used pictures I took of our castle and then had the sharks made special for you," he says. I didn't know he also had pictures, and that warms my heart. He runs his hand through his hair, tousling his dark locks. I like his hair better this way. It suits him.

"I love it. Sharks and sandcastles." I kiss him on the cheek. "It's perfect."

"You're perfect," he says, putting his hand on my cheek.

"We're perfect," I correct him. He nods and brings his lips to mine. We kiss in front of our sandcastle, and I see the flash from the photographer's camera. I'm glad this picture will be mine forever. We are in love, and now we have a picture to hang in our home of sandcastle kisses.

His carefree life is enviable, his kisses are intoxicating, and she can almost imagine a life with him. But all vacations come to an end. And when Cassie invites him to visit her hometown, Wyatt reveals that he can never go back. Not to her town. Not to America. Not to civilization.

Cassie leaves, confused and heartbroken, wondering just who she got herself involved with. Suddenly, her predictable life gets turned upside down when she sees her picture splashed across the Internet. And when the tabloids come looking for the mature woman who found the lost billionaire, she has no idea what to do...

...until he comes back.

Escape With Me: A Midlife Love Story

ABOUT THE AUTHOR

New York Times and USA Today Bestseller Krista Lakes is a thirtysomething who recently rediscovered her passion for writing. She is living happily ever after with her Prince Charming. Her first kid just started preschool and she is happy to welcome her second child into her life, continuing her "Happily Ever After"!

Thank you for supporting an indie author. Anything you can do, whether it be writing a review, or even simply telling a fellow reader that you enjoyed this, helps me out immensely. Thanks!

Krista would love to hear from you! Please contact her at Krista.Lakes@gmail.com or friend her on Facebook!

Further reading:

Bad Boys and Babies
    Family Doctor's Baby
    The Billionaire's Baby Arrangement
    Crime Boss Baby

Kinds of Love
    A Forever Kind of Love
    A Wonderful Kind of Love
    An Endless Kind of Love

Billionaires and Brides

Yours Completely: A Cinderella Love Story

Yours Truly: A Cinderella Love Story

Yours Royally: A Cinderella Love Story

The "Kisses" series

Saltwater Kisses: A Billionaire Love Story

Kisses From Jack: The Other Side of Saltwater Kisses

Rainwater Kisses: A Billionaire Love Story

Champagne Kisses: A Timeless Love Story

Freshwater Kisses: A Billionaire Love Story

Sandcastle Kisses: A Billionaire Love Story

Hurricane Kisses: A Billionaire Love Story

Barefoot Kisses: A Billionaire Love Story

Sunrise Kisses: A Billionaire Love Story

Waterfall Kisses: A Billionaire Love Story

Island Kisses: A Billionaire Love Story

Other Novels

I Choose You: A Secret Billionaire Romance

His Every Desire: A Billionaire Seduction

Wolf Six's Salvation: A Shifter Love Story

Burned: A New Adult Love Story

Walking on Sunshine: A Sweet Summer Romance

An American Cinderella: A Royal Love Story

Mr. Darcy's Kiss: A Contemporary Pride and Prejudice